Emma Dilemma, the Nanny, and the Best Horse Ever

by Patricia Hermes

Marshall Cavendish Children

For Mark Joseph Hermes—at last!

Text copyright © 2011 by Patricia Hermes
Illustrations copyright by Marshall Cavendish Corporation

Other Marshall Cavendish Offices:
Marshall Cavendish International (Asia) Private Limited, 1 New Industrial Road, Singapore 536196 • Marshall Cavendish International (Thailand) Co Ltd. 253 Asoke, 12th Flr, Sukhumvit 21 Road, Klongtoey Nua, Wattana, Bangkok 10110, Thailand • Marshall Cavendish (Malaysia) Sdn Bhd, Times Subang, Lot 46, Subang Hi-Tech Industrial Park, Batu Tiga, 40000 Shah Alam, Selangor Darul Ehsan, Malaysia

Marshall Cavendish is a trademark of Times Publishing Limited.

Library of Congress Cataloging-in-Publication Data

Hermes, Patricia.
Emma Dilemma, the nanny, and the best horse ever / by Patricia Hermes. — 1st ed.
p. cm.
Summary: Emma's happy summer of soccer camp with best friend Luisa and visits to Rooney, the beloved old horse at the nearby stables where Annie the nanny helps out, changes when she discovers that Rooney is being sold and Luisa has some unhappy news.
ISBN 978-0-7614-5905-7
[1. Horses—Fiction. 2. Best friends—Fiction. 3. Friendship—Fiction. 4. Nannies--Fiction. 5. Family life—Fiction. 6. Moving, Household—Fiction.]
I. Title.
PZ7.H4317Emth 2011
[Fic]—dc22
2010042126
Editor: Margery Cuyler

Printed in China (E)
First edition
10 9 8 7 6 5 4 3 2 1

Marshall Cavendish
Children

Other **Emma Dilemma** books:

Emma Dilemma and the New Nanny
Emma Dilemma and the Two Nannies
Emma Dilemma and the Soccer Nanny
Emma Dilemma and the Camping Nanny
Emma Dilemma, the Nanny, and the Secret Ferret

Dad

McClain

Emma

Annie

Lizzie + Ira

Tim

Mom

Contents

Chapter One
Emma's Really Good Horse Plan

It was way past Emma's bedtime-lights-out time, but she was still awake, reading. She had just reached the part in the book where the horse was trying to rescue the little girl. The child had become lost in the desert and was dying of thirst. She had fallen on the ground, fainting from the heat or something and—

"Emma!" It was Mom calling. "Emma! Is your light out?"

Emma quickly reached over to her night table. She switched off the lamp.

"Yes!" she called back. "It's off."

"Okay!" Mom said. "Good night, honey. Sleep well."

"Night," Emma said.

Emma waited a moment. Two moments. Silently, she switched on the lamp. She opened the book.

Just for a minute.

The big horse drummed his hooves on the ground, trying to awaken the girl. "Get up! Wake up," he urged in his horse language, pushing his nose into her face. "You'll die here."

"Emma?" It was Mom again. "You didn't turn that light back on, did you?"

It was so annoying the way Mom could see through walls!

"I'm going to sleep!" Emma called back. "Okay? Okay."

She switched off the lamp again. Really! It would take only five minutes. How could she sleep, not knowing what was going to happen to the girl and her horse?

How could she sleep, anyway? She had so many worries: her sweet, sweet ferret Marshmallow, who acted as if she didn't like Emma anymore, and Rooney, the horse she loved most in the whole world, who was going to get sold and disappear.

Besides all that, it was so darn hot in the house—a hundred degrees, at least, maybe even two hundred. And worst of all, Emma couldn't complain because it was all her fault. She was the one who had wanted the family to "go green." Ever since they had returned from their summerhouse in Maine a few weeks ago, Emma had been thinking about how she could save the earth. In Maine, people were cutting down trees, and the deer had nowhere to hide, and the birds had no place to nest and no nests to put their baby birds in.

It wasn't just trees in Maine. Emma had seen pictures of polar bears up north with no ice to live on so they had to swim hundreds of miles to find mates, and they were always tired.

She knew the earth was home to humans—and she was afraid that humans were ruining it. So at dinner one night, she had suggested that the family "go green" like she had read about, with recycling and stuff. Everyone agreed—Mom; Daddy; Emma's big brother, Tim, who was the best brother in the whole world; the little twins, Ira and Lizzie; and even McClain, Emma's five-year-old sister—and McClain hardly ever agreed to anything.

Annie, their nanny, wanted to help, too. She said she'd make a compost pile out of vegetable scraps and would get worms to eat up the garbage—which Emma thought was kind of weird, but McClain thought was totally wonderful.

The only thing was, Emma had never thought that "going green" would mean no air-conditioning. That's what Daddy said, though. Air-conditioning used up lots and lots of electricity and was bad for the environment. So the whole family had decided it would be all right to give it up. And now, Emma was boiling hot.

Too bad about the environment, Emma thought. But she didn't really mean it.

She plumped up her pillow and lay back. The fan made a nice humming sound, but it didn't cool her one little bit. Her pillow was hot. She turned it over. And over again.

Finally, she threw back the sheet. Mom had said, "Lights out," but she hadn't said, "Don't get out of bed."

Emma went to her window and looked out at the night. Through the treetops, she could just see the roof of the new riding stable called Graybill. It had recently been built on the hill for real horses, not just storybook horses. Real horses like Rooney.

Emma had always loved animals—her two ferrets, Marmaduke and Marshmallow; the family's huge fluffy poodle, Woof; and McClain's fat cat, Kelley, who looked exactly like a stuffed toy, except she wasn't.

But Emma had never been in love the way she was now, with Rooney, a big, beautiful, shiny brown horse with a black mane and tail—the best horse ever. Whenever Emma went to the stables with Annie, Rooney trotted right up to her. He nuzzled her and leaned his body so hard against her at times that he almost knocked her over.

4

"His way of trying to hug you," Annie said.

Annie knew a lot about horses because she had raised horses in Ireland, where she came from. She even knew that Rooney was called a bay because he was brown and black—which Emma thought was kind of weird. If he were a "bay," he should be blue. Except a blue horse would be *really* weird.

When Rooney leaned into her, Emma hugged him back, throwing both arms up and around his big neck. And then, as soon as Annie went into the barn to help Marcus, the stable hand, Emma would sneak into the corral with Rooney. A couple of times, she and Rooney had even gone for a ride. Emma had always looked around to make sure she wasn't being watched. Then, she'd climbed up on the fence rail, grabbed hold of Rooney's mane, and thrown herself onto his back. Rooney had trotted around the corral, 'round and 'round, Emma holding on for dear life.

The second time Emma had almost been caught. It was late afternoon, and Marcus had come out of the barn in his big rubber boots and gone striding over to his little jalopy of a pickup truck. Emma didn't think he'd seen her, because she and Rooney were way down at the far end of the corral, near the meadow, although Marcus had turned toward her briefly. Emma thought Marcus looked a lot like a scarecrow—a kind of mean and grumpy one, skinny and tall, with straw-colored hair that poked out from under the dusty baseball cap that he never took off. Once she had heard Marcus complain to Annie about his truck being temperamental and that one of these days he was going to smash it with a hammer. Emma had watched him from the meadow that afternoon, wondering if this was when he'd really do it. But he didn't.

And then, just a few days ago, the sign had gone up on Rooney's stall: FOR SALE. Rooney's owner had moved away, Marcus had said, and didn't want Rooney anymore. So it was Marcus' job to find a buyer for him.

Emma couldn't imagine anyone not wanting Rooney anymore. She bent over her ferrets' cages, where she had moved them close to the window so they could be cool. Marmaduke and Marshmallow always made her feel better when she was sad. At first, she thought of taking them out of the cages to cuddle, but it was just too hot. Instead, she reached into Marshmallow's cage and patted her nose.

It used to be that Marshmallow would look up happily at Emma. Now, the ferret just turned away, curling herself into a little fur pillow. She'd been acting like this ever since Emma had returned from Maine. Emma knew Marshmallow was mad because of being left behind with a pet sitter, even though the sitter was Emma's best friend, Luisa, who really, really loved Marshmallow. And there was another worry: Maybe Marshmallow loved Luisa more than she loved Emma. Maybe that's why she was acting this way. The thought just about broke Emma's heart.

"Please love me again," Emma whispered. "You and Rooney are both making me so sad."

Marshmallow still didn't lift her head. A kind of nasty smell floated up from the cage. Emma figured that was Marshmallow's way of saying, "Too bad, I'm still mad."

Emma turned and slid a finger into Marmaduke's cage. "You're not mad at me, are you?" she whispered, stroking his nose. "You always love me."

Marmaduke raised his head. He rubbed his nose up and down Emma's finger. He snorted a little, and Emma was pretty sure he said, "Never mad at you! Just sleepy."

He wriggled and started to settle down again. But then he looked up, and his black raisin eyes shone. And he said . . . well, of course, Emma couldn't be sure exactly what he said. But she was sort of sure. Almost completely sure.

He said, "You have some allowance saved up. You could buy Rooney for yourself." Then he shut his eyes and said, "Good night."

Chapter Two
Marshmallow Trouble

In the morning it was much cooler in Emma's room. A sweet little breeze had sprung up during the night, making the curtains puff out from her window a bit. The breeze brought with it just a hint of the horse-barn smell, and Emma breathed in deeply. She loved the smell of horses and hay. She didn't even mind the poop smell too much.

Both Marmaduke and Marshmallow were stirring around in their cages, waking up. In a minute Emma would let them out. But first she had that important something to do before she got ready for her day at camp. Emma and each of her siblings were going to different kinds of camp for the next two weeks till school opened: farm camp for the three younger kids (Annie went with them because the twins were still little), computer camp for Tim, and soccer camp for Emma.

Emma got out of bed and opened her desk drawer where she kept her special stuff, like money and her diary.

She dug around and found what she was looking for—a purse shaped like a kitty's face, where she kept her allowance and gift money. She'd been saving up for a soccer net, but that could wait.

Emma held the purse upside down over her bed and shook it hard. A mountain of coins tumbled out. She fished around with her finger and pulled out the crumpled-up bills.

She sat down on the bed and separated the coins into piles—quarters, nickels, dimes, and pennies. She made small stacks of them. Then she smoothed out the dollar bills and began counting. The dollars didn't take long—seventeen one-dollar bills. One five-dollar bill. And that awesome twenty-dollar bill that Grandpa had sent at the beginning of the summer with a note that said, "Happy Vacation!" Forty-two dollars, even without the coins!

The stacks of coins kept toppling over, so Emma made little groups, counting them out into one-dollar bunches. When she was finished, she found she had fifty-nine dollars and forty-seven cents! She needed only . . . She frowned. . . . Math was not her best subject. Well, spelling and math. She counted on her fingers. She needed only fifty-three cents . . . and then she'd have sixty whole dollars. She could easily find fifty-three cents in pockets or her night-table drawer or somewhere. She didn't think she'd ever had sixty dollars saved before.

Emma didn't know how much a horse cost. Probably a little more than that. Then she thought about Mom and Daddy. What would they say about her getting a horse? She was pretty sure she knew. "No." That's what they'd say. Well, she'd figure out something. Annie would surely help since Annie loved horses, too.

Emma was just starting to gather up the money when her bedroom door burst open. The little twins, Ira and Lizzie, tumbled in, followed by McClain. All three of them leapt onto Emma's bed, scattering coins in all directions.

The twins weren't quite three years old, although they could talk like grownups, practically; McClain was five, almost six; and Emma loved them all to pieces—except for moments like this.

"Farm camp, farm camp!" McClain sang.

"Hugs, hugs, hugs!" Lizzie yelled.

"Me too, me too!" Ira said. He threw himself at Emma. She caught him in her arms, turning her head just in time to keep from getting her nose mashed.

"Careful!" she said. "You're making a mess, you guys! Look what you did!"

They all looked down at the bed.

"What?" Ira said.

"Can I have this nickel?" Lizzie said, holding up a quarter.

"No, you *cannot* have a nickel. Or a quarter," Emma said. She took the coin out of Lizzie's fist. "Now what are you all excited about? What's happening at farm camp?"

"Chickens!" Ira said. "I'm feeding the chickens. Lizzie's helping."

"'Cause Ira's scared of chickens," Lizzie said. "A little. Right, Ira?"

Ira nodded. "Just their feet."

"I'm washing Curly!" McClain said. "Curly's a lamb. Lambs are sheep, did you know that? Curly gets icky 'cause kids sometimes get their lollipops stuck on him."

"And peanut butter," Ira said.

"Ira! Lizzie! McClain!" Mom called. "Time to get dressed. Camp's in less than an hour. Emma, Tim, are you both up and getting ready?"

"I'm up!" Tim called. "I just shut down my laptop."

"I'm up, too!" Emma called back. And then to the little ones, she said, "Okay, scoot!"

They ran out of Emma's room, but McClain turned back. "After camp," she said, "can I go to the horse place, to Graybill's, with you and Annie?"

"No!" Emma said. "You have your own animals at farm camp. Now scoot."

Emma closed the door tightly behind them. She had to let Marshmallow and Marmaduke out for some exercise before she left for soccer camp.

Emma opened up their cages. She picked up both ferrets, kissed them on their little noses, and set them on the floor. Right away, they went scampering about, sniffing and exploring. They did this every morning, hoping that Emma had brought in something new that they could hide inside—or to chew up. Emma had learned to keep important things closed up in her closet or desk.

While they nosed around, Emma got dressed. She pulled on her lightest-weight shorts and the yellow T-shirt that said "Moroney's Soccer Camp" across the front. Emma loved soccer camp. But even better, she loved the time after camp, when she went with Annie to the riding stable.

Although Annie worked full time as their nanny, she'd also begun working a few hours a week at Graybill's where Rooney boarded. Annie was trying to earn extra money to bring her sisters from Ireland for a visit.

Once Annie's boyfriend, Bo, had come along to help, but just once. He'd had a wild sneezing fit that day. His eyes became so swollen he could hardly see, and he'd figured out that he was allergic to horses, which Emma thought was the worst kind of allergy anyone could ever have. Emma didn't mind that he hadn't come along again.

When Emma had her shorts and shirt on, she sat on the side of her bed and pulled on her sneakers. Marshmallow appeared beside her, coming up really close and snuggling. Gently, Emma touched Marshmallow's head. "Does this mean we're friends now?" she asked quietly.

Marshmallow didn't rub her head up and down against Emma's hand in that friendly way she once did. But she didn't pull away, either.

"Good girl," Emma said. "Where'd Marmaduke go?"

Emma looked around and Marshmallow did, too. Marmaduke had scampered to the top of the tall bookcase and was nosing about up there. Marshmallow snuffled at the bed once more, turned around twice, then leapt down and raced away to join Marmaduke.

Emma smiled. At least Marshmallow had cuddled up to her, even if it was only for a moment. She got up and checked her soccer bag. Extra T-shirt, soccer ball, swimsuit and towel, water bottle. Ready to go.

Oops. She was supposed to make her bed. And she had to put her money away. She scooped up the coins that the kids had scattered and put them back in the kitty purse. She picked up the pile of bills. She had folded them so that the twenty-dollar bill was on top. It looked more important that way. But . . . where was the twenty-dollar bill? A bunch of one-dollar bills, the five-dollar bill . . . but no twenty!

Could the breeze have blown it somewhere? No, the curtains weren't moving anymore. Had it become buried in the bed? Emma threw back the covers and felt around. No. Then where was it? She knew the little kids wouldn't have taken it. On the floor? She got down on her hands and knees. No.

She sat back on her heels, frowning, looking around. Marmaduke was still on the top of the bookcase. Marshmallow was beside him.

And sticking out of Marshmallow's mouth—Emma could just see the corner of it—was a twenty-dollar bill. A twenty-dollar bill that Marshmallow was furiously chewing into little, teeny bits.

Chapter Three
McClain Ruins Everything

"Marshmallow, you mean, mean thing!" Emma yelled. "Give that back!"

Emma scrambled to her feet, climbed up on her window seat, reached to the top of the bookcase, almost fell over, and grabbed what was left of the bill from Marshmallow's mouth.

"Bad ferret!" she said. "Bad, bad Marshmallow!"

She jumped down to the floor. She examined the bill. It was all chewed up. Soggy. There was only like half of it left. Tears sprang to her eyes.

Emma ran out of her room, slamming the door behind her. She raced down to the dining room, pounding her feet angrily on the stairs.

The whole family was seated at the table, including Annie. They all looked up, startled. Woof came bounding toward Emma, his ears perked up. "What, what?" he seemed to be asking.

"Whatever is the matter?" Annie asked.

"This!" Emma said. She held out the bill.

"What is it?" Mom asked.

"She ruined it!" Emma said.

"Who ruined what? Come over here, Sweetie," Daddy said, holding out one arm.

Emma circled the table to where Daddy was sitting next to Tim. Daddy wrapped his arm around her waist and pulled her close. "What happened? What do you have there?" he asked.

"It's a twenty-dollar bill," Emma said. "It *used* to be a twenty-dollar bill. It's the one Grandpa sent me for vacation. I need it for . . . for . . . for something important! And Marshmallow ate it! Look!"

"Can I see?" Tim asked. "Maybe it's not ruined."

"Is too!" Emma said, and she pushed the soggy mess toward him. "I was counting my money to see how much I had, and Marshmallow stole it when I wasn't looking."

"It's all right," Tim said, smoothing out the bill. "Know why? There's more than half here. You can take it to the bank and get a new one."

"I can?" Emma said. "They'll let me?"

"Yup," Tim said. He turned to Daddy. "Right, Daddy?"

"Right," Daddy said, nodding. "If there's more than half the bill, they give you a new one."

"They do?" Emma said. "Even if it's soggy and chewed up and disgusting?"

Daddy nodded. "Even then."

"As long as there's more than half," Tim said. "But if there's less than half, then no. Because that way—"

"Oh, I get it!" Emma said. "Because then two people could cut a bill in half and each could get another whole twenty dollars and that would be—it would be—uh, forty dollars? I think. But I'm still really, really mad."

"I'm mad, too!" McClain said.

Emma turned and frowned at McClain, then turned back to Daddy. "Will you take it to the bank for me?" she asked.

"Sure will," Daddy said. He tucked the bill alongside his plate. "I'll do it today. I'll *walk* there. No car. No using gas."

"Thanks, Daddy," Emma said, feeling so relieved. Still, she was really mad at Marshmallow. Marshmallow was so mean sometimes!

Emma slid into her place beside McClain. "What are you mad about?" she asked.

"That!" McClain said, pointing. "Pancakes. Look! They have bugs in them."

"Bugs?" Emma said, peering at the platter of pancakes. "Those are blueberries."

"They look like bugs. And I'm not eating them."

"McClain," Mom said, "they're blueberries, and you know it. Now, if you don't want pancakes, that's fine. You can have yoghurt if you prefer, but you do have to take two bites of the pancakes."

That was the family rule. You didn't have to eat everything on your plate, but you did have to take at least two bites. Also, each kid was allowed just one thing that he or she could always refuse. For Emma, it was lima beans. For McClain and the little kids, it was brussels sprouts. Tim hated mushrooms. He said they were slimy. Tim didn't like anything slimy. He wouldn't even pick up the worms that McClain had started collecting for the compost pile—and kept losing in the house.

McClain shook her head. She didn't pick up her fork.

"McClain," Mom said, "you're going to eat two bites, and you're not going to farm camp until you do. Period. I have to work today, but Daddy doesn't. The twins can go to camp with Annie, and you can stay right here with Daddy. No farm camp for you."

Daddy nodded. "Right," he said.

Daddy was an airline pilot, and sometimes he was gone for a week at a time, and sometimes he was home for a week. This was his home week.

"Un-uh," McClain said. "I'm not staying home.

I'm going. Annie will drive me. Won't you, Annie?"

McClain looked across the table at Annie. Emma did, too. So did Tim and the twins. Tim was frowning. Ira's hand reached out to touch Lizzie's. None of the kids liked it when one of the other kids was sad or in trouble. Even Woof seemed worried, looking from one person to another. He came and rested his head on Emma's knee, and she put a hand on his head.

"Annie?" McClain said again. "You'll take me, won't you?"

Annie fiddled with that pink bracelet she always wore, the one Bo had given her, the way she did when she was worried. It got very quiet as they all watched her.

Annie is the best thing that ever happened to this family, Emma thought. Annie loved each of the kids and all of the pets. She was really young and really, really pretty, and she had great ideas and she laughed a lot and she talked a little funny because she came from Ireland where they had different words for things. She knew how to keep secrets, and she never, ever tattled on anyone. She had her own apartment on the third floor of their house, and sometimes she invited the kids up to play or have tea parties. Even on the days she had off.

There was one thing Emma knew for sure about Annie, though: If Mom said no camp for McClain, there would be no camp for McClain. Except— except lots of times Annie came up with what she called a "splendid idea." Now Emma knew that all the kids were hoping Annie had a splendid idea to get McClain to eat her pancakes. Emma thought that maybe even Mom and Daddy were hoping for it, too.

"Oh, me dear," Annie said quietly at last. "McClain, I know how much you love that wee lamb."

McClain ducked her head. Emma could see that she was trying not to cry.

"And I think that wee lamb might miss you, too," Annie said. "Don't you think so?"

McClain nodded miserably.

"But I might have a splendid idea!" Annie said.

McClain raised her head. Her eyes were shiny with tears just ready to spill over.

"You eat up like your mom said," Annie said. "Two bites. Maybe you could be especially nice and even eat three. Or more."

McClain nodded.

"And then," Annie added, "maybe after camp, you can come to the Graybill barns with me—me and Emma. How would that be?"

Emma felt her heart drop to her toes. Graybill was *her* place! Her special place with Annie. Her special place with Rooney. How could she hug and kiss Rooney and climb up onto the rail and pet him? And maybe even, if Marcus wasn't around, leap onto Rooney's back and ride around the corral? How could she do all that with McClain trailing around after her? She couldn't!

"You wouldn't mind that, Emma, would you, now?" Annie asked. "Just this one time?"

"Yes, I would mind! I do mind," Emma wanted to say. *"I mind a whole lot!"*

But McClain had turned her wide eyes to Emma. Hopeful. Emma could feel the rest of the family watching her, too. Waiting. Hoping.

"Please?" McClain whispered. She folded her little hands in front of her as if she were praying. "Oh, please?"

Emma stared down at her plate. She swallowed. She couldn't make herself say, "Okay." All she could do—she could barely do—was nod.

"Oh, thank you, thank you, oh, goody," McClain said. She picked up her fork and began to eat . . . three bites, four bites, more. She gobbled up the pancakes as if blueberries—maybe even bugs— weren't so bad after all.

21

Emma bit her lip. She had a mean thought. She knew it was a mean thought. But she couldn't help it. And she didn't even try to chase it away. Sometimes, she thought, she really, really wished she were an only child.

Chapter Four

Emma Deserves a Medal

When Emma got to soccer camp that morning, she stood for a minute at the edge of the field, looking around for her friends. Campers were just arriving, their moms and dads dropping them off. Some of the campers were already kicking soccer balls back and forth, waiting for the camp counselor, Mr. Warren, to blow his horrible, squawky whistle for them to line up and check in.

Across the field, Emma saw Luisa, her best, best friend, and Katie, her not-at-all-best friend, kicking a soccer ball back and forth, practicing their footwork.

Luisa was great at soccer, even though she was really tiny and skinny. She had curly, dark hair, and even in the winter, her skin was smooth and tanned. She looked almost like a first-grader, not like the third-grader that she was, but she was super strong. And fast. Katie wasn't great, but she was pretty good—although Emma had a hard time admitting that even to herself. Emma really, really tried to like Katie—or at least, she tried not to hate her. But it was hard. A little while back, Katie had tried to steal Luisa, with Katie and Luisa taking dance lessons together and even having sleepovers at each other's houses like best friends, without asking Emma to come. It had made Emma really mad. Sad, too. Emma and Luisa had made up, though, and now they were best friends again, just the way they used to be. To Emma, that's all that mattered. She didn't care one little bit about Katie, except for trying to avoid her as much as possible. Which was getting hard, because Katie had recently started taking riding lessons at Graybill's.

Now, as Emma watched, two of the other campers, Jason and Jared, darted out onto the field. Jason ran around behind Luisa and stole the ball right from between Luisa's feet.

He kicked it across the field to Jared.

Both boys raced downfield toward the net, Katie and Luisa chasing after them.

Emma dropped her bag by the bench, and even though she was still in sneakers, not cleats, she flew out onto the field. She caught up with Luisa, darting in and out around Jared, trying to get the ball back.

But it was Katie who got the ball—stole it away

from Jared, and with a few quick steps and a mighty kick, drove it into the net.

"Score!" Katie yelled, throwing her arms into the air.

"Not fair!" Jared yelled back, but he was laughing. "It was three against two."

"Not three," Katie said. "Emma didn't do anything."

Which, of course, was totally mean and stupid, but Emma just shrugged. Anyway, nobody seemed to care much about scoring, and they all walked back to the bench together. Katie tossed her long ponytail and didn't even look at Emma.

When they got to the bench in the shade of a tree, Emma and Luisa flopped onto the grass. Katie and Jared and Jason headed for the sign-in table, Katie looking over her shoulder at Emma. Then Katie turned and whispered something in Jason's ear.

Emma made a face at Katie's back.

Even though it had cooled off last night, it was already so hot that Emma could feel sweat dripping off her skin. And it was only nine o'clock in the morning. She pushed her hair back from her forehead. "Why didn't we pick cheerleading camp?" she said.

"Gross!" Luisa said. "I hate cheerleading!"

"Me, too," Emma said. "But they practice in the school gym, and it's air-conditioned. And you know what else? We don't have air-conditioning at home anymore."

"We don't either!" Luisa said. "My dad says it's too expensive."

"My dad says it's bad for the environment," Emma said. "And it's all my fault. I wanted to save the earth—I mean, I still do. I really care about the polar bears having no ice. But I don't see how not using air-conditioning in our house is going to make ice for the polar bears."

"I know," Luisa said. "It's weird."

"Bizarre," Emma said. "But I sort of understand. Daddy says using electricity puts gases and heat and stuff into the air just the way cars do, and that makes the earth warmer all over and—"

And then Emma had a thought—a brilliant thought. Of course! The answer to her dilemma. The thing Mom and Daddy couldn't say no to. She sat up straight.

"Luisa!" she said. "Listen! You know how I go to Graybill's barns with Annie? And you know how I've told you about Rooney?"

Luisa nodded. "Yeah?" She had rolled over onto her stomach and was picking at the grass. She was always looking for lucky four-leaf clovers.

"Rooney's going to get sold," Emma said. "Marcus put the sign up on his stall just the other day."

"Oh, no!" Luisa said. She sat up. "No!"

"No, no, it's okay!" Emma said, "because I am going to buy him."

"You are?" Luisa stared at Emma. "Really?"

Emma nodded. "Really."

"Your parents are buying him for you?"

"No!" Emma said. "*I'm* buying him. Well, I think I'm buying him. I haven't told my parents yet. But they'll have to say yes. And you know why?"

"Why?"

"Because horses don't need gas!"

Luisa rolled her eyes. "Duh!"

"No, not 'duh'! Listen. Horses don't use gas so they don't do anything bad to the environment."

"They poop," Luisa said.

"Yeah, but that's good for the environment. Did you know that? Some people even buy horse poop."

"Do not."

"Do too. They use it as fertilizer. Well, I think they do. Maybe it's cow poop. Anyway, Mom and Daddy could give up one of our cars in exchange for Rooney! We could—I could—ride Rooney to soccer practices and everything. It would be perfect. One horse. One less car to mess up the environment. So how can they say no to that?"

Luisa shrugged. "'Cause parents say no to everything."

"Well, yeah," Emma said. "But not to this. They can't!"

"A horse," Luisa said. She sighed. "You're so lucky. My parents won't even let me get a ferret. They say it costs too much."

"Ferrets don't cost that much," Emma said.

"That's what I told them," Luisa said. "But they say it's not just the ferret, but the cage and food and vet bills." Luisa sighed again and used this weird kind of mimicking voice. "'This is too expensive, that's too expensive.' They say that about everything. Ever since my dad lost his job, all they talk about is money. I think they even fight about it."

"Oh," Emma said. She looked away. Her own parents hardly ever argued, but once in a while, she could tell they were grumpy at one another. Emma hated it when that happened. Luckily, it didn't happen too often. And it never lasted long. Emma was also happy that both Mom and Daddy had jobs.

Luisa was blinking hard and picking at the grass again. Her hair was plastered to her head with sweat, and she looked so little. And so sad.

"Well," Emma said. "Ferrets aren't all that great anyway. I mean, they can be a pain. This morning, guess what Marshmallow did? She almost chewed my twenty-dollar bill to pieces."

"Marshmallow didn't do anything mean to *me* when *I* had her all summer," Luisa said.

Emma didn't think that was a very nice thing for Luisa to say. But after a minute, Emma went on anyway. "Ever since I left her with you, she's been mad at me. She won't even snuggle up to me anymore or crawl inside my shirt like she used to."

Luisa opened her mouth. Emma was suddenly sure she knew exactly what Luisa was going to say: "Marshmallow snuggled up to me all summer." But Luisa didn't say that. She just closed her mouth and didn't say anything at all. And she looked downright tragic.

Emma bent her head. She began picking at the grass, too.

After a minute, she looked up. Luisa still seemed miserable.

"Want to sleep over this weekend, maybe Friday?" Emma asked. "You can hold Marshmallow all you want."

"Oh, yay!" Luisa said. "I'll ask my mom, okay?"

"Okay," Emma said. Then, because she was feeling very generous all of a sudden, she added, "You can even sleep with Marshmallow if you want. And you know what else? When I get Rooney, I'll let you ride him, too."

Just then, Mr. Warren blew his horrible, squawky

whistle, and Emma and Luisa jumped to their feet. Luisa was smiling as she grabbed Emma's arm and pulled her toward the sign-in table.

Emma drew in a big breath. Some days, it seemed she did nothing but get herself into trouble. But today, between McClain and Luisa, she'd done nothing but good.

She really, really thought she should get a medal.

Chapter Five
A Riding Lesson

The only thing was, nobody gives medals to kids. At least, nobody had ever given one to Emma. But that afternoon, as Emma sat beside McClain in Annie's car on the way to Graybill's, Emma imagined what it would be like to get a medal.

She imagined a big fire up at the horse barns. Annie had told her that because hay caught fire easily, you had to be really careful about fire near horses and barns. Horses were very, very terrified of fire. So Emma made this big fire inside her head, flames shooting up out of the top of the barns, and she saved every single horse, all by herself.

She imagined covering Rooney's eyes with one hand, so he wouldn't see the fire, and leading him with the other. She put him in the corral and closed him in. Then she ran back and got the rest of the horses. One horse tried to race back into the barn, because horses did that sometimes, Annie said, even if the barn was on fire. So Emma grabbed him by his mane and held on till she had him safely closed up in the corral, too.

When the president heard about it, he called her up. He invited her to the White House to give her a medal. He said he'd send his private plane for her, *Air Force One*, and she could bring her family, too.

Emma said she'd be honored, and yes, she'd bring the whole family, including Annie.

Except maybe not McClain.

Emma looked over at McClain now. McClain was bouncing up and down in her booster seat, leaning forward to talk to Annie. McClain never stopped talking. She was absolutely going to ruin this whole afternoon, and Emma wouldn't be able to ride Rooney and she'd have to hold McClain's hand the whole time.

But when they got to Graybill's, that didn't happen at all.

"Oh, no, me dear," Annie said when McClain was ready to run off with Emma. "I'm not going to do my work while you're here. I'll just spend an hour or so with you both and come back tonight to help Marcus finish up."

Emma frowned. "But you always work when I'm here."

Annie smiled. "But that's with just you. Not with McClain here."

Annie looked toward McClain, who had already run across the path and climbed up on a fence. She was leaning over it, reaching down to pet a little shaggy pony that was on the other side nibbling grass. She was leaning over so far, it looked as if she might fall into the corral headfirst.

"McClain's a wee bit of a handful, is she not?" Annie said, smiling.

"She's a wee bit of a pain!" Emma said. But she said it quietly.

McClain was a pain, and not just a wee one, either. Still, Emma didn't want to hurt her feelings. Although . . . Emma wouldn't let her come to the White House.

"Now, where is that Rooney of yours?" Annie said.

They both looked around.

Rooney wasn't out in the meadow with the other horses or in the corral. That meant someone was either riding him or else he was in his stall in the barn. Or . . . Emma caught her breath. Marcus hadn't sold him already, had he?

"Annie!" she said. "I'm going to go in the barn and look. He's there, right?"

Annie seemed to know what Emma was thinking. "I'm sure he is," she said. "It's hard to sell a horse.

Surely Marcus didn't find a buyer for him this fast."

Emma ran to the barn, her heart beating hard inside her chest. Once in the barn, Emma had trouble adjusting her eyes to the dark after the bright sun outside. She had to slow down a bit so as not to trip. "Oh, don't be gone, don't be gone," she whispered as she made her way between the stalls.

Rooney wasn't gone. He was right there, right in his stall, his big head and neck stretching out over the bottom part of the door. He was weaving his head back and forth, back and forth, as if he were doing a slow kind of dance.

"Rooney!" Emma yelled. She jumped up onto the door's crossbar, ready to throw her arms around his neck.

And then she noticed—Rooney wasn't alone in the stall. Marcus was there, too. He had a bit and bridle in his hands and was about to put them on Rooney.

When Marcus saw Emma, he nodded but he didn't say hi or anything.

"Oh," Emma said. She suddenly felt shy, even a little nervous. She remembered how Marcus had threatened to bash up his old pickup truck. Did he know she had stolen a couple of rides?

"Hi," Emma said, since she felt as if she should say something.

Marcus nodded again but still didn't speak. He just eased the bit into Rooney's mouth and secured the bridle. Emma felt very proud of herself for knowing the names of all the horse equipment. Annie had been teaching her, and Emma had even been studying up in a book Annie had given her. Emma knew that if Marcus was doing these things, it meant he was about to ride Rooney. Or someone was.

Someone who had come to buy Rooney?

Emma swallowed hard. She couldn't make herself ask. She just stood there watching, feeling her heart pounding.

Marcus turned, threw a blanket over Rooney's back, and went to the rear of the stall. He lifted up a saddle. He held it in both hands, as if weighing it. He nodded at Emma.

"Come on in here," he said. "We'll see if it fits."

Emma frowned at him. "What?"

"You!" he said. "Try this saddle."

"But I . . . but I don't take lessons or anything," Emma said.

Marcus closed his eyes. He opened them. He sighed.

"I mean, I can't pay you or anything," Emma said. "I mean, my parents didn't—"

"You want to ride? Or not ride?" he asked.

"Oh, I do, yes, I really do!" Emma said.

"Then get in here," he said. "I seen you. Two different times. Going bareback around the corral like a wild one. I know how it is. When I was your age, I thought saddles were for sissies, too. But if you're going to ride, you may as well learn to do it right. And not break your neck."

Emma felt her face get red. So he had seen her after all! She was so embarrassed. She looked down at her feet for a minute. She chewed on her lip. She looked up. She was so, so embarrassed.

She was.

But not so embarrassed that she'd say no.

Chapter Six

Happiness

Emma wondered if you could die of happiness.

Rooney was still there. He hadn't been sold. And Emma was actually going to ride him. The right way. Saddle and all. And she wouldn't even have to sneak a ride in the corral, like she had before.

She went into the stall and watched as Marcus threw the saddle up onto Rooney. It looked as if it was heavy. Marcus tightened the girth, the strap that went under Rooney's belly and kept the saddle tight on his back.

Marcus stepped away. "Now," he said, "here's the first thing you need to learn. Watch!"

Emma didn't know what she was supposed to be watching. But Marcus was looking at Rooney, so Emma looked, too. After a minute, Rooney sort of snickered, letting his breath out in a big, fat horse sigh.

"See what he did?" Marcus said. "When he sees me coming with the saddle, he sucks in a big breath. He holds it so his belly gets fat. That way, I can't make the girth tight. So you got to wait till he blows his breath out. Then you tighten the girth again. Else the saddle falls sideways and you fall off!"

"He's smart!" Emma said.

"Sure is. Whoever buys him is getting a real smart horse. He don't spook easy, either. Only thing he's afraid of is rats. Then he acts up, wild as a mustang. I make sure there's no feed in his stall, so the rats stay away. Mostly. Queer, too, since there're plenty of rats around a barn and most horses get used to 'em."

"Yuck!" Emma said. "You mean there're rats here?"

Marcus frowned at her. "'Course there're rats. It's a barn. If you got a barn and feed and horses, you got rats. You ain't scared of a little rat, are you?"

Emma looked toward the corners of the stall, kind of nervously. Yes, she was scared of a little rat. Big ones, too. Were they really hanging around? She knew some rats were friendly. In the pet store, where she bought Marmaduke and Marshmallow's food, she had even seen pet rats for sale. And in a book she had read about Charlotte, who was a spider, there was a rat who was kind of mean but not horrible or anything. He was a barn rat, too. Emma had a feeling that real barn rats were different, though.

She definitely didn't want to meet one.

Marcus bent to tighten the girth some more, then stood up and patted Rooney's rump hard. "He's a good lad, he is. Almost human. A whole lot easier to work with than a car or a truck."

Emma remembered again how Marcus had said he wanted to smash his pickup. "You need a new car or truck?" she asked.

"Sure do. Don't know that I'll ever get one, though."

And then Emma had her second brilliant thought of the day. "My dad might be getting rid of his car soon."

"That right?" Marcus said. "What kind of car is it?"

"Uh, a gray one," Emma said.

Marcus gave her a kind of disgusted look, then shook his head. "Brilliant!" he muttered.

He squinted at Rooney. "Looks okay," he said. He made a cradlelike shape with his hands, weaving his fingers together. He held them out to Emma. "Hop up!" he said.

Emma stepped onto his hands, and Marcus gave her a hoist up. Once she had settled into the saddle, Marcus adjusted the stirrups, finding just the right length for Emma's legs and feet. He also handed Emma a helmet to put on.

Marcus stepped back, studied Rooney some more, studied Emma, then bent again to make some more adjustments.

While Marcus did that, Emma sat up straight. She was so happy she could hardly believe this was real. She was getting a riding lesson, a real one. She was on top of Rooney; a saddle was beneath her; she was wearing a riding helmet like a real horseback rider. She was holding the reins, holding them loosely the way she had read she should. Her feet were in the stirrups. She could feel the warmth of Rooney against her legs, his big breath puffing, his sides going in and out, in and out. Emma breathed along with him, deep, happy breaths.

After a minute, Emma couldn't stand the happiness anymore. She dropped the reins. She leaned forward. Out of the corner of her eye, she could see that Marcus was watching her. So what? She bent and wrapped both arms around Rooney's neck, hugging him tight, tight, tight, burying her face in his mane.

Rooney made a happy, nickering sound.

Emma straightened up. She slid a sideways look at Marcus. He was still watching her. She had to bite her lip to keep from smiling. A ridiculous thought had suddenly popped into her head: *If it wasn't so embarrassing,* she thought, *I just might have hugged Marcus, too.*

Chapter Seven

Horse in Danger

Well, poops on this, Emma thought. What a dumb, stupid way to ride a horse.

Marcus had led Emma out of the barn and into the corral, where Annie and McClain were still fussing over the little shaggy pony. Marcus rode his horse, Denver, with a lead rope attached to Rooney. Once inside the corral, Marcus stayed in the middle, holding one end of the rope in his hands, the other end attached to Rooney. He made Emma ride 'round and 'round in a circle.

It was okay. It was fun having Annie cheering her on and McClain clapping her hands and squealing. It was fun for Emma to feel that she could control and hold onto Rooney.

But it was dull.

It was boring. It was horribly, terribly bor-ing!

Emma wanted to fly, fly the way she had flown

on Rooney bareback. She wanted to feel the wind blowing her hair wildly, feel the sun on her back and neck, feel how Rooney's body got hot from the sun and warmed Emma's legs, and how the wind made her eyes water, and the way she and Rooney felt like one person. Or maybe, one horse.

Instead: *Trot, trot, trot.* Walk around in a circle. Trot some more. *Bounce, bounce, bounce. Walk, walk, walk.*

Finally, after they had gone around the corral a hundred million times, Emma tugged gently on the reins, and Rooney immediately responded. They slowed to a halt, right in front of Annie and McClain, who were still by the corral fence.

Emma was kind of out of breath, surprised at how much work it was to make Rooney do what she wanted him to do. But she was doing it, and she was good at it, she could tell. Now, if only she could get out of the stupid, boring corral.

"You're a natural!" Annie said, reaching over the fence and patting Rooney. She smiled up at Emma. "Look at you. You must have some Irish blood in those veins. Wait till me sisters come. You can maybe teach them a thing or two."

"I want to ride, too!" McClain said. "Can I? Please, please, please?"

"Rooney's too big for you," Annie said. "Tell you

what. I'll let you ride the pony in a minute. Okay?"

"Okay," McClain said.

Emma thought it was kind of weird that McClain agreed so quickly not to ride Rooney. McClain usually fussed till she got what she wanted. But Emma also thought maybe McClain might be a little scared of Rooney. Rooney was awfully big and he probably seemed even bigger to McClain, since she was so little.

Annie turned to Emma again. "You're a natural, me dear," she said. "You don't even bounce in the trot!"

"I do a little," Emma admitted. "It makes my bottom sore. But wait till you see me gallop. That's easy."

Emma tugged gently on the reins so that she and Rooney turned to face Marcus.

"Can we go out in the field now?" she asked. "Or along the trail?"

Marcus shrugged. He turned to Annie. "You think she's ready?" he asked. "I'd hate to see her break her neck."

Annie laughed. "I think she's part horse herself. What do you think, Emma?"

"Let's go!" Emma said.

"Okay," Marcus said. "But we're going to start out slow. No galloping yet!"

And they did start out slow. Too slow. But within minutes, Emma had dug her heels into Rooney's side, and she and Rooney began trotting along the trail, out into the meadow, and down along the rock-wall, Marcus following behind on Denver. From the rock wall area, Emma could look down the hill and see part of her own backyard, the trampoline gleaming greenish-blue in the sun.

Free, free, free! The wind rushed past her, and she started to dig her heels harder into Rooney's side. She wanted to gallop, faster and faster, the way she had done bareback. But Rooney seemed to sense that maybe he should go slowly because he actually turned his head, looking behind at Denver and Marcus. Emma thought he was checking with Marcus. "Is it okay to go faster?"

Marcus seemed to hear the unspoken words.

"You just take it slow, young lady!" Marcus said. "Trotting is plenty for your first time out. Don't you even think of putting him in a gallop or you'll never get on him again."

"Okay, okay!" Emma said.

But she did urge Rooney into a faster trot. She felt the clopping of Rooney's hooves, the warmth of him as he swayed right beneath her.

Annie is right, Emma thought. *I am definitely part horse.*

Emma didn't know how long they rode—trotting, then slowing to a walk to let Rooney cool off, then trotting again. But soon—too soon—Marcus said it was time to turn back. They had been out for a whole hour, he said.

An hour!

It felt like minutes. But since Emma wasn't paying for this lesson or this ride, she didn't argue.

When they got back to the corral, they cooled down their horses, walking them slowly, while Annie and McClain came to walk alongside.

McClain was popping up and down like a little puppet. "I rode saggy pony!" she said. "I rode saggy pony."

"Shaggy pony," Emma said.

"That's what I said," McClain said.

Emma dismounted while Annie held the reins. Emma was surprised at how sore she felt. Especially her bottom and the insides of her legs.

Annie helped Emma take off Rooney's tack and saddle while Marcus said nice things to Annie about Emma's riding ability, things that surprised Emma and made her happy.

And then Marcus said something horrible, something truly, terribly horrible.

"Got to get Rooney all spruced up come Saturday,"

Marcus said. "Some folks from Pennsylvania are driving up to take a look at him."

Emma sucked in her breath. "They are?" she said. Her voice came out in a helpless kind of squeak. She cleared her throat. "Why? I mean . . ."

"They got a kid—Oliver, or some oddball name like that," Marcus said. "They want a horse for him, and they don't mind that Rooney's old. If Rooney's as good with Oliver as he is with you, them parents will be real happy."

"So will Oliver," McClain said.

Marcus laughed, the first time Emma had ever seen him smile. He was missing a couple of teeth.

But Emma wasn't smiling. Neither was Annie.

Marcus shrugged. "Not sure they'll buy him, though. Kinda hope not. I've gotten awful used to him. I told his owner—fussy lady, Ms. Adams—ain't easy selling an old horse. She can't expect to get much for him."

Annie wrapped an arm around Emma's shoulders. Emma was pretty sure Annie knew just what she was thinking. And feeling.

Desperate.

And though Emma hadn't even met Oliver, she hated him a whole, whole lot.

Chapter Eight
Emma Causes a Flood

It took a little while for Emma and Marcus and Annie to get the horses cooled down and set out to pasture and the tack put away. But eventually they were finished.

As soon as they had all clambered into the car, Emma said, "Annie? How much does Rooney cost, do you know?"

"No, me dear," Annie said. "I don't know. I didn't ask."

"I did," McClain said.

"You did?" Emma said, turning to look at McClain. "You asked Marcus?"

McClain nodded.

"What did he say?"

"I forget," McClain said.

"You forget?" Emma said.

"I think he said a hundred dollars. Or a thousand,"

McClain said. "Well, maybe not a thousand. 'Cause he's old. I mean Rooney's old. Not Marcus. Well, he's old, too."

"Big help," Emma muttered. But it really didn't matter. Even if it was a hundred dollars, all she had was sixty.

Annie had started up the car and was pulling out of the drive. She looked at Emma in the rearview mirror.

"Emma, dear," Annie said. "You're not thinking of trying to buy Rooney, are you?"

"*Of course I am.*" But Emma only said it inside her head.

Out loud, she said, "No! Just wondering."

Which, of course, was not at all the truth. But she couldn't say anything with McClain sitting right there. If McClain knew Emma wanted to buy Rooney, McClain would instantly run and tell Mom and Daddy. And there was a right way and a wrong way to ask for something. Emma had found that out a long time ago. A right time and wrong time, too.

"I'm glad to hear that," Annie said. "I wouldn't want you thinking about it because Rooney needs a home. But he needs a good one. With plenty of room to roam. Not just a regular yard or anything."

"I know that," Emma said.

She didn't know it, though. She could absolutely, positively take better care of Rooney than stupid Oliver could. And she had to do something soon. Saturday was just two days away!

They drove silently the few blocks home. Once there, Emma jumped out of the car and flew to her room. She closed her door tight, let the ferrets out to play, and sat down at her desk. She needed her diary. She had started writing in it earlier in the summer. She wrote down stuff that happened and important things to remember, like what to say to parents when you wanted something really, really badly.

Emma dug through her desk drawer looking for the diary—hair clips, ponytail holders with hair stuck in them, barrettes, a yo-yo, some doll shoes. A bunch of doll socks. Oh! And there was that trick thing that you put your fingers in and it closed them in tight. And there was the lock that needed a magic key to open it, but the key was lost. A battery. She wondered what that was for.

And then she found it. Her diary.

She turned the pages. There was a page about the time she had hidden her ferret in her backpack—two times, actually. There was a page about telling the truth. Emma mostly always told the truth although sometimes she did exaggerate. And there was that

50

page she had written a few weeks ago, about how sometimes people seemed really mean but turned out to be not so mean after all. Emma looked out the window at her new tree. She thought about Mr. Thompson, the man in Maine. Mr. Thompson had been kind of mean at first, but then he had turned out to be kind of nice. He had even had that tree planted for Emma.

Next Emma thought about Katie. Katie *seemed* kind of mean. And she *was* mean.

Emma found the page she'd been looking for. She read her rules over to herself:

Be puhlite. Do not yell. Or cry.
Don't ask a favor wen parents are grumpy or Mom has a
     head ake.
Or wen Daddy is away on his plane. Daddy says yes. Mom
     always says no.
Don't ask wen McClain is having a tempur tantrum.
Or wen the twins are throwing up.
Or wen Woof is chasing Marshmallow and Marmaduke
     around the dining rum table.

Emma frowned at the pages. She wasn't very good at spelling, so some of the words looked weird. Still, it was a good list. The little kids hadn't been sick, so they wouldn't be throwing up tonight.

McClain was happy because she'd ridden shaggy pony, so she probably wouldn't have a tantrum.

Daddy was home.

Emma would be sure to keep her ferrets closed up in her room.

Perfect.

Tonight. At dinner. Unless Mom had a headache. Which she probably wouldn't since everybody had been gone at camp all day.

And then Emma had one more thought. Mom and Daddy liked it when Emma did chores and stuff without being asked. Emma knew she needed a bath or shower tonight. She was really dirty and smelly from soccer and from Rooney and riding. She'd take a shower before dinner and surprise Mom and Daddy.

She went into the bathroom with clean undies and pajamas, undressed, and got into the shower.

Too bad she forgot to close the shower door tight. Because she spent a long, long time in the shower, letting the hot water run over her. She knew that part of "going green" was not using too much water. But her legs were really sore and so was her bottom, and the hot water felt so, so good.

When she was finished, she stepped out—into a huge puddle of water! Water was inches deep all over the bathroom floor—like really, truly deep.

The bath mat was actually floating a little.

Oops. Emma would have to add that to her list—"Don't make a flood." But it was okay. All she had to do was sop up the water on the floor with the bathroom towels. She did, but then she needed a few more towels, so she got an armload from the linen closet in the hall. Actually, the water had leaked out under the door and into the hall, so she mopped that up, too. It took about ten towels to soak up all the water, but finally the floor was dry. She stood back and looked at it. Perfect. Cleaner than it had ever looked.

She slung the wet towels into the bathtub.

Now, dinner. And the most important talk she'd ever, ever have.

Chapter Nine
McClain Ruins Everything.
Again.

Spaghetti for dinner! Perfect. All the kids liked spaghetti, so nobody would fuss about not wanting to eat.

Mom seemed relaxed, and so did Daddy. The sky was getting dark, as if a thunderstorm was coming, and a breeze was blowing through the open windows. That made the house cooler and made everyone happier. Emma had already asked if Luisa could spend the night on Friday, and Mom had said yes, certainly.

"And you know what else, honey?" Mom said. "I am so proud of you for getting bathed before dinner without being told."

"I really stunk," Emma said.

Daddy laughed. "We're still proud of you."

Mom put her hand over Emma's hand on the table, patting it lightly. She smiled.

"You are getting to be so grown up, do you know that?" Mom said.

"I am?" Emma asked. "Really?"

Mom nodded.

"I am too," McClain piped up.

Mom smiled at McClain, then turned back to Emma.

"Really, Emma," Mom said. "I see you being so much more responsible. Not that you haven't always been, but . . . well, lately, you seem more responsible. More grown up in many ways."

Emma ducked her head. It felt good to know Mom thought that. And it would help. Mom would see how responsible Emma would be caring for a horse. For Rooney.

"I see that, too," Daddy said. He was down at the other end of the table, cutting up the spaghetti into little bits for the twins.

He looked at Mom. "And you know what?" he said. "They're all growing up. Too fast, I think. Before we know it, they'll be grown up and gone, the five of them."

Well, Emma hoped not. She didn't think she wanted to be a grownup—at least, not yet. Grown-ups had to go to work and cook dinner and bathe little kids and cut up their spaghetti and meat and change their icky diapers. Emma was glad the twins had grown out of the diaper stage, at least.

"I'm already almost grown up," McClain piped up. "So can I get a pony?"

"*What?*" Emma said.

"A pony?" Daddy said, laughing. "No, you cannot get a pony."

"McClain!" Emma said. "You are so mean! I want a pony—I mean, a horse—and you know it. I want Rooney."

Daddy just shook his head.

Mom shook her head, too. She rolled her eyes at Daddy. That usually made Emma mad, except Emma was so mad at McClain, there was no more mad left over.

Tim frowned, looking from Emma to McClain.

Ira clapped his fat little hands.

So did Lizzie. She also knocked over her milk. "Yea, yea, yea!" she cried. "McClain, can I ride your pony?"

"Me, too?" Ira said.

"Yes, you can. Ira, too!" McClain said. "Ponies aren't big. Rooney's a monster big horse."

"Stop it, McClain!" Emma said.

"Stop, stop, stop," Daddy said. He dropped a cloth napkin in front of Lizzie's place, soaking up the milk. The family had stopped using paper napkins in order to help save the earth, so now they had to constantly wash a bunch of cloth napkins. Emma wondered if that really made sense, using up water and soap and the washing machine.

Daddy turned to Emma, then McClain. "Listen," he said. "Listen carefully. Nobody is getting a horse. Or a pony. Understand that? Nobody. No horse. No pony. We have a dog. We have a cat. Emma, you have two ferrets! Wherever did you get this wild idea from?"

"From Annie," Emma said.

"Annie?" Mom said. "Annie suggested this?!"

"Well, not exactly," Emma said. "In fact, she said I probably shouldn't even think about it. But she did sort of mention that Rooney needed a good home." Emma glared at McClain. "And Annie didn't say anything about a stupid pony, McClain!"

"He's not stupid."

"Girls!" Daddy said. "Enough. Emma, Rooney is a horse, I take it?"

"Not just a horse, Daddy!" Emma said. She jumped up and ran to the head of the table. She leaned against Daddy's chair, and Daddy put his arm around her waist. "Rooney is the best horse in the world. I visit him when I go to Graybill's stables with Annie. You know how they offer lessons and rides? Marcus—he works there—he let me have a ride today for free! I love Rooney so much and he loves me back, I can tell. And now his owner wants to sell him, and somebody might come buy him Saturday, some kid—"

"Oliver," McClain said. "The kid's name is Oliver."

"Hush up, McClain!" Emma said.

"Halt!" Daddy said, holding up his hand like a traffic cop.

Daddy pulled Emma more tightly against him. He kissed her cheek. "No, sweetheart," he said softly. "No, no, no. I understand you want him. But we have plenty of pets, and a horse or even a pony is out of the question."

"But Daddy! I'd pay for him and everything. I've got sixty dollars saved. Marcus said Rooney wouldn't cost much 'cause he's kind of old—Rooney, I mean, not Marcus. Anyway, you and Mom both just said how responsible I am. . . ."

Daddy and Mom were shaking their heads. Mom had her eyes closed, like she was shutting out this whole conversation.

"But, Daddy!" Emma said.

"No!" Daddy said.

"Listen," Emma said. "Just for a minute?"

"I'll listen," Daddy said. "But the answer is still no."

"Okay," Emma said. "Listen, I figured it all out. See, we could keep him in the backyard. Or in that field between our house and Luisa's. Maybe you could build him a stable and—"

Daddy laughed.

"It wouldn't have to be a big stable," Emma said.

"'Cause ponies are little," McClain said.

Again, Emma glared at McClain. "Just something to keep him out of the rain," Emma went on. "And—"

"No," Daddy said.

"No," Mom said.

"But listen!" Emma said. "This is the important part—we could sell one of our cars!"

"We could *what*?" Daddy said.

"Sell one of our cars and get Rooney instead!" Emma looked from Mom to Daddy. "I know how you care about gas and air-conditioning and all that stuff that's hurting the environment. So if we had a horse—if we had Rooney—instead of a car, we would be saving the environment. I could ride to soccer practice and we could ride to the store and maybe even to church and everything. Right?"

"Hey!" Tim said. "Know what? That's a good idea."

Emma smiled at Tim. He was the sweetest brother in the whole world—especially considering that he was a little scared of horses. Actually, Tim was a little scared of lots of things. Like the thunderstorm that might be coming.

Mom just rolled her eyes again, resting her head against the back of her chair. And then she frowned. "What's that?" she said.

"What?" Daddy asked.

"That!" Mom said. She was looking up at the ceiling in the corner of the dining room by the hall doorway. A big, dark stain had spread across one corner. Emma thought it looked like the shape of a horse.

Daddy stood up. He went to stand below the stain. "Hmm," he said. "Looks as if we have a leak."

"It's not raining," Tim said. "Not yet."

Daddy looked out the window. "No," he said. "It's not raining. That's the hall bathroom above there, isn't it?" He turned to Emma. "Emma, did you have a problem with the shower earlier? Is that the bathroom you used before?"

"Uh-oh," Emma said.

Chapter Ten
Absolutely. No. Horse.

No, Emma could not get a horse.

No, McClain could not get a pony.

Too expensive, too much work, too ridiculous, too blah, blah, blah. No horse. No pony. Period.

McClain had her usual temper tantrum and ran upstairs to lock herself in her room.

As she stamped up the stairs, Mom called after her, "And don't start banging things around up there, you hear?"

Like that did any good. In about a minute, the house was practically shaking as McClain banged something against something else.

Mom and Daddy exchanged looks.

Emma fought back tears. She didn't know who she was madder at—Mom or Daddy or stupid McClain. If McClain hadn't started with that pony business, Daddy just might have said yes. Emma had thought it all out ahead of time. She had planned everything so carefully.

Well, mostly carefully. There was that business of the flood. But Emma had cleaned that up. It really wasn't that bad. All they'd have to do is paint the ceiling a little bit. At least, that's what Mom had said they could do after the ceiling dried out. But Daddy said that it might stay wet, and then they'd need the plasterer. That would mean a mess. And money.

Still, Emma wasn't giving up on Rooney. Not yet. Even though McClain had run upstairs to have her tantrum, Emma was determined to try once more. This was just too, too important. If Rooney got sold on Saturday . . . well, Emma couldn't even think about that.

"Daddy!" Emma said, very quietly, calmly, not at all like McClain—just like the really responsible daughter that she was. "Mom? Daddy? Just listen to this. About the car. And the horse. And the environment."

Daddy acted as if he didn't even hear her. He was frowning at the stain on the ceiling.

"It could be good for the environment, Daddy," Tim said. "Emma's right about that. Especially if we get rid of one car."

Daddy didn't answer.

Emma sent a thank-you look to Tim.

Upstairs, the banging went on in McClain's room. The twins had become very quiet. They were holding hands, the way they did when they were worried. It had begun to rain, just lightly, the rain running in little rivulets down the windows.

Daddy closed his eyes. He breathed hard through his nose, like a dragon.

Bad sign.

"Tim?" Daddy said very, very quietly. "Emma? End. Of. Conversation."

"Won't you let me say one more thing?" Emma said.

"No!" Daddy said.

"Well, I think you and Mom are both really, really mean!" Emma said.

She jumped out of her chair and ran up the stairs, too, stamping angrily. Halfway up, she stopped. *"I hate you, you stink,"* she said. *"You're like the Grinch. But worse. Stink. Stank. Stunk. You are the meanest parents in the whole, entire world."*

That's what she said. But she didn't say it out loud. She just said it inside her head. She still meant it, though. She meant it very, very much.

Chapter Eleven
A New Plan

Once in her room, Emma slammed her door hard. She thought she knew exactly how McClain must feel. Because Emma felt like banging stuff, too.

But she wouldn't. She wouldn't be as stupid and childish as McClain. She'd be grown up. She'd be responsible. And she wouldn't give up. She was going to get Rooney. Somehow.

Emma looked around for her ferrets. They were still loose in her room, and she found Marshmallow sleeping on top of a pile of shoes by her bed. Emma picked her up and cradled her, snuggling her close.

"I'm so mad and so sad," she whispered in Marshmallow's ear.

Marshmallow didn't look up sweetly at Emma. She didn't try to crawl up inside Emma's pajama shirt the way she used to. She didn't even lean against Emma's shoulder. She just turned her head away, as if she wanted to be left alone.

"And *you're* not helping much!" Emma said.

She plopped Marshmallow down on the floor, maybe a little too hard. *Well, poops on you,* Emma thought. It was too hot to snuggle anyway.

Emma looked around for Marmaduke. He was sitting up, looking at her from the window seat, like he was waiting to talk to her.

Emma went to the window seat, sat down, and lifted Marmaduke onto her shoulder. She held him so he could look out the window. It was raining harder now, and there was a rumble of thunder, too. *Poor Tim,* Emma thought. *He really hates thunder and lightning storms.*

McClain did, too. Sometimes both McClain and Tim came creeping into Emma's bed during storms. *But if McClain shows up tonight,* Emma thought, *too bad! McClain can go right back to her own bed and be scared there all by herself.*

"You understand about Rooney, don't you?" Emma whispered, holding Marmaduke close. "It was your idea that I buy him."

Marmaduke nodded. He snuggled up against Emma's shoulder, then turned himself around and crawled inside her pajama shirt, wriggling about till his little head popped out the top.

"Mom and Daddy are so super mean," Emma whispered.

Marmaduke nodded again. His shiny black eyes looked right into Emma's. Emma was pretty sure he said, "I know." And then he put his little face right close to hers, asking to be kissed again.

Emma kissed him, then sat a while, cuddling him, just thinking.

She had no idea what to do. Mom and Daddy were absolutely, positively not going to let her get Rooney. Oliver was coming on Saturday. And like Marcus said, if Rooney was as nice and gentle with Oliver as he was with Emma . . .

And then an idea began to grow inside Emma. It wasn't a perfect idea. In fact, it wasn't even a nice idea. But if Rooney wasn't sweet and gentle, if he acted up, wild as a mustang . . .

No. That wouldn't be right. Still, it was a possibility. And then, another thought came. A better thought. One that wasn't naughty. A splendid idea!

What if Annie bought Rooney? That way Rooney could keep on living at Graybill's, just as he did now. He wouldn't have to move into their backyard and have Daddy build a stable for him. Emma would give Annie sixty dollars to buy him!

Of course, he might cost more than that, maybe

a lot more, but Emma could save her allowance to pay Annie back. Her sixty dollars could just be a "down payment." Daddy had explained what that was when Emma had seen an ad on TV about buying a car. It meant you paid a little money at first, a down payment, and you got the car—or the horse—and you paid the rest later when you had enough money. So as Emma got more allowance, she could keep giving it to Annie until Rooney was all paid up.

But all this had to happen soon—tomorrow. Oliver was coming on Saturday.

Emma knew that Annie would be home from Graybill's any minute. She had gone back before dinner to do the work she hadn't done that afternoon because of McClain coming along. Emma would stay awake. She'd tiptoe up to Annie's apartment and tell her the plan. The kids weren't supposed to go up to Annie's without permission, but Emma sometimes did. And Annie never minded.

Emma took a deep breath. She hugged Marmaduke. "I have an idea!" she whispered. "I think it's a good one, too."

Marmaduke looked up at Emma. Emma was pretty sure he said, "I'm sure it's a splendid idea!"

And then, because it was getting kind of late, Emma put both ferrets back in their cages. It was getting dark, too, and the rain was coming down even harder. The room was much cooler. Emma closed her window so the rain wouldn't come in.

She went to her bed, threw aside the top sheet, and lay down. Since she was already in her pajamas, she didn't have to get ready for bed. All she had to do was brush her teeth.

Nah, forget it. Her teeth wouldn't fall out if she skipped this one time. Anyway, she wasn't going to go to sleep yet. She'd just read a little bit while she waited for Annie to come home. Maybe she'd get up later and brush her teeth.

Suddenly, Emma had a worrisome thought— sometimes Annie came home with Bo. Emma hadn't liked Bo much at first, because he took up too much of Annie's free time, time that Annie used to spend with Emma. Now Emma was kind of used to him, although she was glad that he was allergic to horses. She even liked him a little bit, maybe because Annie did. Still, Emma hoped he wouldn't hang around tonight.

Emma picked up her book, *The Secret Garden*. That and *Anne of Green Gables* were Emma's two favorite books in the whole world. Emma had read both of them a zillion times, because she loved them so much. *The Secret Garden* was a good book for when she was feeling sad. Mary, in the book, had been sad a lot, too. Her parents had died! But then Mary met this kid who was a pain at first, but soon they became best friends, and they discovered a secret garden together.

Emma read a few pages. She was really tired, though, and her eyes kept closing. She was exhausted from soccer camp and from riding Rooney and from being mad at McClain. She was extra exhausted from being mad at Mom and Daddy for being so mean, and from being worried that Rooney would be sold to Oliver.

And then, next thing Emma knew, it was pitch dark in her room and Daddy was bending over her. She felt him move her book off her tummy and set it on her night table. He brushed her hair off her face. He adjusted the sheet, pulling it up over her shoulders. Then he bent and kissed her forehead.

"Good night, sweetheart," he whispered.

He started to tiptoe out of the room.

But Emma said, "I'm awake."

Daddy turned. "Hey," he said. He came back in and sat down beside her on the bed. "I didn't mean to wake you up," he said softly.

"You didn't," Emma said, even though he had. She sat up. "Daddy?"

"What, sweetheart?"

Emma just sighed. She slumped back against her

pillow. A flash of lightning lit up the room. "Oh, never mind," she said.

She had planned to ask about Rooney again. But she knew better. She knew plenty about her parents by now, and she knew when something was a lost cause. "Nothing," she said.

"Emma, honey?" Daddy said. "Annie came home a while ago. She told us what a great horsewoman you are and how well you rode today."

Emma nodded. "I'm pretty good."

"So," Daddy said, "Mom and I were thinking—maybe you could take riding lessons. You might have to give up some other things, dance or soccer. We don't want you overscheduled. But would you like to do that?"

Emma shrugged. Yes, she would like to. She loved horses. But she loved Rooney most of all. And it was Rooney she wanted. No other horse in the world. But that thought was only inside her head. Out loud, she said, "I guess. Maybe." And then she added, "Annie's home?"

Daddy nodded.

"Is Bo with her?" Emma asked.

Daddy laughed softly. "No. I think she and Bo had a little tiff."

"What's that?" Emma asked.

"A little quarrel. Bo thinks Annie's spending too

much of her free time with horses."

Ha, Bo! Emma thought. *Now you know how I feel!* Still, Emma felt a little bad about the "tiff"—especially for Annie.

"Is Annie sad?" Emma said, sitting up straighter.

"Maybe a little," Daddy said. "But don't you worry about Annie. She'll be fine. Just think about what I said. We can talk about it in the morning—riding lessons, I mean."

Emma nodded and slid down under the sheet. She wasn't going back to sleep, though. She would sneak up to Annie's apartment the minute Mom and Daddy went to bed. And if her parents would really let her have riding lessons, and if Annie really bought Rooney, then Emma could ride Rooney all she wanted.

Except . . . well, Emma knew things didn't always work out the way she wanted.

Lightning lit up the room once more, and Emma could see Daddy's face clearly. He was smiling down at her, and he brushed her hair from her face again. She couldn't help herself. She had to ask one more time. "Daddy?" she said.

"What, sweetie?"

"I really can't get a horse? Get Rooney?"

"You really can't get a horse," Daddy said. "But think about riding lessons. Okay?"

Emma sighed. She remembered what she had thought about Mom and Daddy before—that she hated them, that they stunk, that they were the meanest parents in the whole, entire world.

They weren't, though. They were just—well, just *sort of* mean. "I don't hate you, Daddy," Emma said.

"That's good," Daddy said, bending and kissing her again. "Because I love you to pieces."

Chapter Twelve

A Thunderstorm

Emma waited. And waited. She could hear Mom and Daddy still moving around, could hear the TV in the background. She sat up straight so she wouldn't fall back asleep. She slid her book under her butt so she'd be uncomfortable. A couple of times, she pinched her arm. Then, she started shaking her hands hard, so hard her fingers snapped against one another.

Wouldn't they ever go to bed? Emma was so sleepy.

Finally, though, finally, things got still. From under the crack in her door, Emma saw the lights go out and the hall get dark.

She waited just a little bit longer. Then, quietly, she crept out of bed. She found her frog slippers and slid her feet into them. Even though it had cooled off some, it was way too hot for slippers.

But she loved her frogs. The frogs were kind of like Marmaduke: They sometimes gave Emma good ideas or encouragement. When she wiggled her feet, the frogs frowned as if they were worried. Other times, when Emma wiggled her toes, the frogs nodded yes at her if she had a good idea. But sometimes, they just looked plain blank.

Emma opened her door and peered down the hall. No light was coming from under Mom and Daddy's door. The whole house was quiet.

Woof was lying just outside Emma's room. He scrambled to his feet when he saw her.

"Hush," she warned him. She put a hand on his head. "We're going to visit Annie."

Quietly, Emma tiptoed down the hall, Woof trotting alongside her. His nails made clicking sounds on the wood floor. The door that led up to Annie's apartment was at the far end of the hall. A light was coming from under the door. Annie was still awake! Emma tapped lightly. She listened.

No answer.

She tapped again. Then she opened the door just a crack.

"Annie?" she called. She didn't like to go up without being invited. She knew that was rude. Annie needed her privacy. That's what Mom and Daddy always said.

But Woof didn't worry about privacy or being rude. He leapt past Emma and up the stairs, his collar jingling.

"Hey, Woof!" Emma heard Annie say. And then Annie called, "Emma, is that you?"

"Yes, it's me," Emma answered. "Can I come up?"

"But of course, me dear."

Emma went scooting up the stairs. One of her frog slippers fell off, but she didn't bother to retrieve it. She just shook her other foot hard till that slipper fell off, too, and tumbled down the steps.

At the top of the stairs, Emma turned toward the sofa where Annie often sat, reading or watching TV.

Annie was there. But she wasn't reading. Or watching TV. And she wasn't alone.

Tim was on the sofa with her. Also, McClain. Also, McClain's cat, Kelley.

McClain was sound asleep, her thumb in her mouth, her mass of curls tumbling around her face. Her face was kind of streaky-looking from tears. Kelley was sleeping on McClain's feet.

"Come on, join us," Annie said. "But let's not wake the little one." She patted the sofa beside her, moving over a bit so Emma could squeeze in between her and McClain.

"Why's everybody up here?" Emma asked quietly.

"McClain was scared of the storm," Annie said.

"Oh," Emma said. But McClain always came to Emma's room in a storm. McClain must have known that Emma was really mad at her. Emma wondered if she'd have let McClain in. She ducked her head. She felt kind of bad.

"Me, too," Tim said. "I went to your room, but you were asleep. Your book was on your tummy. I didn't want to wake you. I knew you were sad."

"Oh," Emma said again.

Annie put her arm around Emma. "Emma," she said. "Tim told me what happened at supper. I'm so sorry."

"But Annie?" Emma said, looking at her. "I had a new idea. Could you buy Rooney maybe? And keep him up at Graybill's?"

"Oh, no, me dear," Annie said. "I don't have near enough money to buy a horse."

"I do. I have sixty dollars," Emma said. "I'll give it to you. I know he'll cost more, but—"

"Oh, honey," Annie said. "He costs way, way more than that."

"I know," Emma said. "I know that! But I was thinking we could make a down payment."

"Oh, honey, I don't think so," Annie said.

"I have an idea!" Tim said. "I read about

racehorses and how sometimes a bunch of people own a horse together. Maybe you could find a bunch of people to chip in and you could all own Rooney together."

A funny thought popped into Emma's head. How did you decide who owned the head of the horse and who owned the feet and the tail and all the rest?

"Oh, no," Annie said. "Even if we had the money to buy him, even if a bunch of us did it together, do you know what it costs to keep a horse?"

"What do you mean?" Emma asked.

"To feed him and pay stable fees and vet fees and shoeing and everything else?" Annie said. "All that work that Marcus does?"

Emma shook her head.

"A lot of money," Annie said. "A really, really lot of money. Why, I believe those people who board their horses at the stable—like that Ms. Adams who owns Rooney—they pay about two thousand dollars a year. Maybe even three."

"Three thousand? Every year?" Emma asked.

Annie nodded. "Every single year."

Emma collapsed back against the sofa.

"You know what?" Annie said. "We're together. Even if we're all a little sad. Tim doesn't like storms. McClain wants a pony that she's not getting. You're not getting Rooney. But . . . but if we're together,

77

we're not so sad. Right?"

Wrong. Emma looked down at her lap. Something else was wrong. She knew, even though Annie hadn't said so.

"You're sad, too," Emma whispered. "Daddy told me." She looked at Annie. "Your eyes are all red."

Annie sighed. "Right," she said. "I'm a little sad, too. That I am."

Emma bit her lip. She felt guilty for having been happy earlier when Daddy said Annie and Bo had had a fight.

Emma put her head on Annie's shoulder. Gone. Emma's dream was gone. McClain's dream was gone. Maybe even Annie's dream boyfriend was gone. Emma looked down at McClain and put a hand on her curls.

The only one who could be even a tiny bit happy now was Tim. The storm had begun to move away, the thunder no more than a little rumble now and then.

"Let's just snuggle," Annie said. "Shall we?" She rested her head on top of Emma's. She put one arm around Tim and one around Emma and pulled them in close to her. Woof came over and lay down by Emma's feet, and Emma dug her bare toes into his curly fur.

Kelley woke up and inched her way onto Emma's lap.

Then the whole bunch of them, sad and sleepy and disappointed, fell sound asleep. Together.

Before they did, though, Emma heard Annie whisper, "Don't worry, me dears. Things will be better in the morning."

Chapter Thirteen

Losing a Best Friend

And they were better.

A little bit anyway. It was Friday. Luisa was going to sleep over. And Emma had woken up in the night with another brilliant plan for Rooney that just might work. She knew she couldn't buy Rooney. She knew Annie couldn't buy and care for him. But there was a way Emma could keep Rooney from being sold. The next day. Or any other day. If it worked out.

Rats. Rooney was scared of rats. He got wild as a mustang when he saw a rat. That's what Marcus had said. So if Rooney saw a rat, he wouldn't be nice and mild with that Oliver kid, especially if the rats were in his stall. Not that Emma would actually put a rat in Rooney's stall. She wouldn't. Even if she could, she wouldn't. But what if Rooney saw a *ferret* in his stall?

Ferrets did look a little bit like rats, if you didn't know better. The O'Fallons had once had a nanny who didn't know better. The first time the nanny saw Marmaduke running around in the house, she had yelled, "A rat! A rat!" And she'd tried bashing him with a shovel.

Rooney was probably smarter than that nanny, though—Horrid Nanny, the kids had called her. Still, in the dark of the barn, it would be pretty hard for even a smart horse like Rooney to tell the difference between a rat and a ferret.

The only thing was, would Emma really be doing something wrong? She felt a little worried about her idea. But then she decided not to worry. Because thinking about doing something bad was not the same as doing something bad.

Especially since she wasn't *definitely* going to do it.

Late that afternoon, Emma sat out on the back steps with both ferrets in her arms, waiting for Luisa to arrive for their sleepover. Earlier, Emma had gone to Graybill's with Annie when soccer camp was over, but Emma had left after about five minutes. Marcus wouldn't let her anywhere near Rooney. Oliver's family was coming first thing in the morning, Marcus said, and he didn't want Rooney all wound up and excited. All "wilded up," Marcus called it. He wouldn't even let Emma visit Rooney in his stall.

81

Now, Emma hugged Marmaduke and Marshmallow close against her chest. They were wearing
their harnesses that were attached to their leashes.
Emma had promised Mom that she'd keep them
leashed the whole time she was outside. But now
Emma had an idea. Once Luisa arrived, she and
Luisa could get the old playpen out of the garage
that the twins used when they were toddlers. Mom
and Daddy used to take the playpen to Emma's
soccer games and plop the twins inside it. It was
made out of mesh stuff, not slats or bars. Emma
and Luisa could put the ferrets into the playpen.
Marmaduke and Marshmallow could play inside it
but still be outside, not cooped up in the house.
They'd be safe. And they couldn't get away.

It was very quiet that afternoon, both outside and
inside the house—and it was taking Luisa forever
to get there! Daddy had taken Tim to the computer
store. Annie had put all three little kids in the wagon
and pulled them into town to the dollar store—in the
wagon, not the car, because of the environment.
Each kid had a dollar for having done chores all
week without complaining, and they were dying to
spend it. Mom was the only one home, and she was
working in her office in the back of the house.

Marshmallow and Marmaduke lifted their heads,
sniffing the air and wriggling their noses, so happy

to be out in the open. Emma knew they wanted to run free, to sniff out stuff on their own. But she had promised.

"Not today," she whispered to them. "I promised Mom. But tonight. In the barn. Maybe."

Emma frowned and looked toward Luisa's house. What was taking Luisa so long? She lived directly behind Emma, but there was a long, long field and a creek between the two houses. Emma glanced at the Mickey Mouse watch that Tim had given her for her birthday. Luisa should have been there over an hour ago.

Finally, finally, Emma saw Luisa coming. Luisa had her backpack hung over one shoulder and her pillow tucked under one arm. Luisa always brought her own pillow for sleepovers because she said she couldn't sleep without her fluffy pillow. It didn't look very fluffy to Emma. It looked more like Woof's beat-up doggie bed.

"At last!" Emma said. She stood up and went partway down the lawn to meet Luisa. "What took you so long?"

"Stuff!" Luisa yelled. "Just stuff. Parents!"

She said *parents* like it was a dirty word.

Luisa scrambled up the slope to Emma. As soon as she got close, she dropped her pillow and backpack onto the grass.

Luisa stuck her fists into the pockets of her shorts. She glared at Emma. "So guess what?" she said. "Mom and Daddy just told me. We're moving!"

"You're *what*?" Emma said.

"*Moving!*" Luisa said again. "We can't afford the house anymore since Daddy lost his job, and so we're moving!"

"Moving where?"

"Somewhere."

"When?"

Luisa shrugged. "Soon. I mean, not like next week or anything but pretty soon. Mom and Daddy are having a garage sale tomorrow to start emptying out the house."

"But you can't move!" Emma said. "You can't! You're my best friend."

"I know," Luisa said. "I'm so mad. Why can't we just stay a while longer? Daddy will get a job soon." She ducked her head, and Emma could see that she was fighting back tears.

Emma was blinking away tears, too. It was so unfair. Luisa had no home anymore. What was Emma going to do without her best, best friend right next door?

Luisa had turned away and was looking toward her house. She rubbed her fists across her eyes.

"Here," Emma said softly. "Here." She held

Marshmallow out to Luisa. "You can hold her for a minute."

Luisa turned back. She rubbed her fists across her eyes once more. Her face was kind of streaky with tears, but she smiled. "Thanks," she whispered. She took Marshmallow into her arms.

Emma watched worriedly. Would Marshmallow cuddle with Luisa? Emma hoped not. But at the same time, she hoped so. She felt sad for Luisa.

Luisa buried her face in Marshmallow's fur. "I've missed you!" she said. "I've missed you so, so much!"

Marshmallow wriggled around. She looked up into Luisa's face. Then Marshmallow pressed her head against Luisa's shoulder and let it lay there, all quiet and snuggly like.

Just the way she used to do with Emma.

"You are so adorable!" Luisa said, hugging Marshmallow closer and laughing.

"Stop!" Emma said. "Cut it out! You're squishing her!"

"Am I? I am not. I mean, I didn't mean to," Luisa said. She held Marshmallow up and looked into her face. "I've just missed her. A lot."

"Well, it's not like you haven't seen her for a year or anything," Emma said.

Emma knew she sounded mean. She just couldn't help it.

"I know," Luisa said. "It's just that . . . you know."

Yeah, Emma did know.

Because Marshmallow raised her head again. This time, she stuck her nose up and pressed it right against Luisa's mouth, asking for a kiss.

Emma turned away.

"Should we take them up to your room?" Luisa asked.

Emma shook her head. "They're happier outside. I had an idea before. The little kids' playpen. It's in the garage. We can put them in there. Come on. I'll show you."

Together, they started up the lawn toward the house. Luisa carried Marshmallow and her pillow. Emma carried Marmaduke. Emma also picked up Luisa's backpack for her. Emma tried not to be mad at Luisa. Or Marshmallow. Or Luisa's parents.

When they got up close to the house, Emma said, "We have to tie these guys up for a minute while we get the playpen out of the garage."

"Why tie them up?" Luisa asked. She nodded toward the back of the house. "We could just put them in there for a minute, couldn't we?"

She was looking at the enclosure where all the ugly stuff lived—garden hoses and trash pails and the air-conditioning motors and vents and lots of junk. Daddy had built the enclosure so you couldn't see how messy everything was. There was a gate that closed it up, too, so that the raccoons and skunks couldn't get into the garbage pails. Although they did sometimes anyway.

Emma frowned. "Nah. I mean, yeah, we'll put them in there, but we still have to tie their leashes onto something. Otherwise, they'll flatten themselves out and creep right under the fence."

Emma opened the gate to the enclosure. She saw the hose spigot inside. She wound Marmaduke's leash around it a couple of times. She tugged at it. Fine. Nice and tight.

Luisa attached Marshmallow's leash to the dryer vent that stuck out from the basement wall. "This okay?" she asked.

Emma nodded.

Perfect.

They closed the gate and went to the garage.

Emma found the playpen and showed it to Luisa. "See? We'll put Marshmallow and Marmaduke in here."

"They won't get out?" Luisa asked, frowning.

"How can they?" Emma said.

Luisa shrugged. "'Cause it's mesh or something. They'll chew right through."

"Not with us watching them," Emma said. "Trust me. Come on."

Together, she and Luisa lugged the playpen out of the garage. They set it up under some trees, where it would be cool. When it was all set up, Emma tested it by leaning against it. It didn't wiggle or give way. Then Emma walked around it, checking for holes in the mesh. None.

"Perfect," she said.

"I don't know," Luisa said, sounding worried.

"It's fine!" Emma said. "Really. They can't get out." She smiled at Luisa. It wasn't Luisa's fault that Marshmallow liked Luisa better than she liked Emma. *If* Marshmallow *did* like Luisa better. Which Emma hoped she didn't.

And it wasn't Luisa's fault that she had to move. Besides, maybe tomorrow or the next day or the next, Luisa's mom or dad would find a job and then they wouldn't have to move. Then everything would be okay again.

"Come on, let's go get them," Emma said.

They went back for the ferrets. Emma opened the gate. She bent to untie Marmaduke. He was happily sniffing at the garbage cans.

Luisa bent to untie Marshmallow.

The only thing was—Marshmallow was nowhere to be seen!

Chapter Fourteen
Marshmallow Gets Stuck

Well, that wasn't exactly true. Emma could see Marshmallow—at least, Emma could see a part of her. Her scraggy tail and her butt were sticking out of the hose from the dryer vent. But as Emma watched, even they disappeared.

Only the leash was left sticking out.

"Oh, no!" Luisa said. She grabbed the leash and tugged on it. "Come on, come out of there!" she said.

Marshmallow didn't come out.

Luisa pulled harder. "Come on!" she said.

Nothing.

"No! Stop! You'll hurt her! I'll get her!" Emma said.

"She's stuck!" Luisa said.

"She can't be," Emma said. "Move over. Let me try."

Luisa backed up. Emma knelt down and peered into the fat, white plastic hose. There was a small metal cover over the opening—or there had been. But Marshmallow had pushed it aside. Now Emma could see her way down inside the hose.

"Come on, Marshmallow," Emma said. Gently, she tugged on the leash. "Come on. Back out. You can do it."

But Marshmallow either didn't want to or couldn't. She absolutely did not budge.

"Okay," Emma told her. "I'm going to pull you. It won't hurt."

She was very glad she had bought harnesses for both ferrets instead of just leashes and collars. If it were just a collar leash, she'd be choking Marshmallow to death. Emma pulled a bit harder.

Nothing.

Marshmallow still didn't budge. Her little feet scrabbled against the hose, but the rest of her didn't move at all. Not even an inch. She was snuffling, breathing hard.

"Okay, okay, don't worry," Emma said. "Let me get my hands on you."

Emma let go of the leash. She slid both hands inside the hose, trying to grab hold of Marshmallow's little furry body. But Marshmallow was wedged too tightly. There was no room for Emma's hands and arms—well, not for both hands. She could get just one hand around Marshmallow, but even so, she couldn't pull her out.

"Let me try!" Luisa said. "My arms are littler than yours. So are my hands. Is she breathing, is she okay?"

"She's breathing," Emma said. "But she's not okay. She's really stuck."

Emma was a little bit scared—no, she was a lot scared. What if she couldn't get Marshmallow out?

Luisa moved over to the dryer opening, elbowing Emma aside. "Come on, let me see," she said. She shoved her face into the vent. Practically her whole head disappeared. Only her thick, dark curls poked out, and her skinny little bottom pointed up in the air.

After a minute, Luisa backed out, too. "She's really stuck," she said.

And then Emma had a thought. "I know what," she said. "You pull on the leash. I'll grab as much of her as I can get my hands on. If we both pull together, she might pop free."

"But don't pull her by her tail!" Luisa said.

"I won't," Emma said. "I'll get her by her tummy. If I can."

Emma switched places with Luisa again, then turned to the hose opening. She put her arm in, just one arm. She managed to get her fingers curled around Marshmallow's tummy. She squashed Marshmallow carefully, trying to make her smaller.

"Okay," she said over her shoulder to Luisa. "I have her. You ready?"

"I'm ready," Luisa said.

"*Now*," Emma said.

Emma pulled. And squashed.

Luisa tugged.

Nothing.

Marshmallow didn't move, not even an inch. She just made a huffy sound. Emma knew she was saying, "Would you please get me out of here?"

Behind Emma, Marmaduke was making huffy sounds, too. Emma knew he was worried. They were all worried.

Emma sat back on her heels. She had an awful picture in her head of Marshmallow stuck there forever and the dryer blowing hot air on her all the time. Which wouldn't be too bad in the winter but could be horribly awful in the summer. And besides, Marshmallow would starve to death in there.

"I know what!" Luisa said. "We can push her right into the dryer. I'll give her a little shove, and you run into the basement and just take her out!"

Emma shook her head. "Won't work. I asked Annie once how the hot air got out of the vent.

She said there's a fan and a screen or something in the back of the dryer, and it keeps mice and stuff outside from getting inside. We'd have to take off the back of the dryer."

Luisa bit her lip. "Should we get your mom?" she said. "Or Annie?"

Emma shook her head. "Annie's not here. And Mom will kill me."

"The fire department?" Luisa said.

"Mom would really kill me," Emma said.

And then Emma had an idea. A brilliant idea.

"Stay here!" she said, jumping to her feet. "I'll be right back. Keep talking to Marshmallow. Marmaduke, too. They're both scared."

"Where are you going?" Luisa asked.

"I'll be right back. You'll see," Emma said.

Emma ran into the house and up the stairs to the bathroom. She knew exactly what she needed. Once, McClain had stuck her thumb into the top of a baby doll's bottle. When she couldn't get her thumb back out, she had begun yelling, "Call the fire department, call the fire department!" Why McClain had thought the fire department would help, Emma had no idea.

But Annie had calmed McClain down. Annie just ran cold water over McClain's thumb and the bottle. And then she used baby oil to make McClain's thumb slippery. After just a minute or two, McClain's thumb popped right out, although her thumb stayed kind of red for a while.

Emma wouldn't pour water on Marshmallow. But the baby oil might work. Not only that, Emma knew baby oil was great for cleaning ferrets, even better than water, sometimes. She looked around for it. In the medicine cabinet. Under the sink. In the shower. The linen closet.

No baby oil.

Now what?

And then she saw it—right on top of the hamper. A large plastic bottle of baby oil. She grabbed it, ran downstairs, and circled around to the back of the house.

Luisa's face was pressed against the dryer vent, and she was talking to Marshmallow.

"Okay, move over," Emma said.

"What do you have?" Luisa asked.

"Baby oil."

"*Baby oil?*" Luisa said. And then she said, "Oh. I get it."

Emma knelt down. She opened the bottle of baby oil. She poured a whole bunch of it onto her hands. She rubbed her hands together till they were all slippery and gooey.

She put one hand into the vent, reaching way in till she could touch Marshmallow. She rubbed her hand all over Marshmallow's body—or as much of Marshmallow as she was able to reach. She backed up and poured more baby oil on her hands. And then she had an even better thought.

She turned the bottle upside down in the vent. The baby oil poured out. Emma used both hands to spread it around. She took a deep breath and backed out a little, wiping her hands on her shorts.

"Think it will work?" Luisa said.

"It will. It has to," Emma said. "I'm going to pull her while you tug on the leash like before. But wait till I tell you I have a hold of her."

"Okay," Luisa said. "And I'm going to pray, too."

Emma turned back to the hose. She reached way in till she got one hand around Marshmallow's slimy tummy. "Ready?" she said over her shoulder.

"Ready," Luisa said.

"Go!" Emma said. She squeezed Marshmallow carefully but firmly. She tugged.

Luisa tugged.

And Marshmallow popped out of the vent like a little cork. She landed right at Emma's feet, perfectly okay, although she looked a little confused.

She also looked disgusting. Her fur was slippery

and slimy, flattened along her back so that her backbone stuck up.

Hmm, Emma thought. *She really does look a lot like a rat.*

Chapter Fifteen
Nighttime Trip to the Horse Barn

It was the middle of the night. All the lights in the house were out.

The twins had been tucked in bed. McClain had ceased her chattering; she talked nonstop, even in bed, ordering around her dolls and stuffed animals, or sometimes, if she was in a sweet mood, singing to them. But now she had become quiet.

Mom and Daddy had long since gone to bed.

No light was peeping out from under Annie's door.

And Emma and Luisa were standing at the back door, preparing to tiptoe out of the house. They were heading for Graybill's—to get Rooney all "wilded up." They had both ferrets in their arms, leashes and harnesses attached.

Very, very softly, Emma turned the lock on the back door. It made a big, fat clicking sound.

Luisa sucked in her breath.

"It's okay," Emma whispered. She pushed on the door. The back door was weird—it opened outward instead of in, and it was creaky. But it was the best way to get from the house into the back field. Unless someone was looking out a window—which they weren't—Emma and Luisa would never be seen.

Very gently, Emma put both hands against the door and pushed. It gave a few inches, squeaking on its hinges.

Luisa sucked in her breath again.

"Don't worry," Emma whispered. "Mom and Daddy can't hear anything. Their bedroom's in the front."

"Good thing," Luisa whispered back. "If they catch us, we're in big trouble."

"If they catch us, we're dead," Emma said. "Now come on."

She opened the door the rest of the way, and they stepped outside into the moonlight. The moon was full and so bright that Emma could see her shadow. It felt spooky, but nice spooky. Still, she felt exposed out there in the light. "Let's walk under the trees," she whispered.

Luisa nodded.

Silently, they crept out into the yard, staying close to the line of trees. To get to Graybill's, they had to walk down Emma's back lawn, across the field between Emma's house and Luisa's, through Luisa's backyard, and then up the path through the woods. Once up the hill, they could see the horse barns right ahead.

Neither of them spoke. As they passed through Luisa's yard, they were extra quiet and careful, trying not to let even a branch or twig move under their feet. All the lights were out in Luisa's house, too.

A sad feeling welled up inside Emma again. Luisa would be leaving that house and moving away soon.

Except Emma had another idea.

Once they had crossed Luisa's yard and started up the hill, Emma finally felt able to breathe once more. Even though she had told Luisa that no one would see them, she'd been a little bit nervous.

"Luisa?" Emma said quietly. "I have an idea. Why don't you come live with us? We have a big house. You could share my room. We could have so much fun."

"I'd miss my parents," Luisa said.

"No!" Emma said. "I mean your whole family! Couldn't your mom and dad move in, too? We have a spare bedroom for guests."

"I don't think so," Luisa said slowly. "I mean, where'd we put our furniture and stuff?"

99

"I don't know," Emma said. "But we could ask Mom and Daddy. Maybe you could put everything in the garage. Or something."

"I don't think so," Luisa said again. "Mom said that if Daddy doesn't get a job soon—or if she doesn't—we'll go live with Grandma. But for now, we'll just rent a smaller house or an apartment somewhere."

"But doesn't your grandma live in—in, like, Guadalupe or something?" Emma asked.

"Silly!" Luisa said. "I've told you a zillion times—*Guatemala*."

"Oh," Emma said. She had no idea where Guatemala was—or Guadalupe, for that matter—except that they were far, far away.

"So where's the place you're renting?" Emma asked.

"We don't know yet," Luisa said. "Probably not around here, though. Daddy says this area is too expensive. But maybe close enough that I can still go to our school."

"You *have* to go to our school!" Emma said.

"That's what I told Daddy," Luisa said. And then suddenly, she cried, "Ouch!" And she tumbled onto the ground. Marshmallow went spilling out of her arms.

Instantly, Emma threw herself forward, hoping

to catch Marshmallow. She landed facedown, Marmaduke still clutched tightly to her chest. Luckily, both she and Marmaduke had fallen squarely on top of the other ferret.

Emma sat up, clutching both ferrets in her arms. "Sorry, Marshmallow," she whispered. "Didn't mean to squash you. Again. You okay?"

Marshmallow nodded.

Emma turned to Luisa. "You okay?" she said. "What happened?"

"I tripped!" Luisa said. "A tree root or something." She got to her feet. She brushed at her knee. "I'm okay," she said. "It's not bleeding. Come on. Let's get this over with and get home. I can't believe I let you talk me into this. We're going to be in so much trouble."

"Only if we get caught," Emma said, getting to her feet and handing Marshmallow back to Luisa. Marshmallow nosed her way into Luisa's shirt. "And we're not going to."

"Ha!" Luisa said.

"Stop worrying," Emma said quietly. "Now come on. Follow me."

"You sure nobody's around?" Luisa asked. "Like a night watchman or something?"

"Oh," Emma said. She stopped. She had never thought of that. But then she shook her head. Annie or Marcus or someone would have said so.

"Nah," she said, "there's no one. Marcus lives in a little house back there, way behind the barns. But it's far back. He'll be asleep, too."

"You hope," Luisa said. And then she added, "I hope."

By then, they had reached the top of the hill. The horse barns loomed ahead, quiet in the moonlight. As they got closer, Emma could hear the shuffling and breathing of the horses.

"Okay," Emma said, clutching Marmaduke to her chest. "Stay right behind me. There're some tiny little lights inside. But look where you're stepping. Sometimes there's horse poop. Okay?"

"*Horse poop?*" Luisa said. "Gross."

"Just be careful where you step, that's all."

Silently, they tiptoed into the barn, Emma first, Luisa following.

It was really quiet inside. Some horses had their heads sticking out of the stalls. Some were sleeping standing up. All was still, except for the shuffling of hooves, the swishing of tails. And breathing. Lots and lots of heavy horse breathing.

Emma stopped outside of Rooney's stall. She stood on tiptoe and peered inside. Rooney was asleep, stretched out flat on the floor. He looked like an enormous horse rug. Emma stood for a moment, watching him, hugging Marmaduke to her. And beginning to worry.

"What?" Luisa whispered.

"I just thought of something," Emma whispered. She turned to Luisa. "I was going to put Marshmallow and Marmaduke down in the stall. But I'm scared. Because of what Marcus said. About how wild Rooney gets. What if Rooney steps on them? He could trample them to death."

Luisa sucked in her breath.

"I'll wake Rooney up," Emma whispered. "We can just *show* them to him. Maybe just seeing them will work."

But Rooney didn't need to be awakened. He had heard Emma's voice. He hauled himself to his feet. In a minute, he was at the door of the stall, his big old head raised, looking right at Emma. He reached far out of the opening, trying to press his head against Emma's, ready to give her his horse hug and kiss.

And then he saw Marmaduke. And Marmaduke saw him. Marmaduke stuck his head up, tilting it side to side, wriggling it back and forth as if he were trying to say hello.

Rooney didn't want to say hello. He whinnied loudly. He backed up into his stall. His eyes rolled around wildly. He began breathing in little snorts.

"I'll show him Marshmallow," Luisa said.

Emma nodded. But suddenly, she felt terrible. Rooney was scared. What they were doing to him was so mean. He began turning himself 'round and 'round in his stall, as if trying to get away. Then, as Emma watched, he began banging against the walls of the stall.

"It's all right, it's all right!" Emma told him, leaning over the edge of the door. She held Marmaduke down near her waist, out of sight.

To Luisa, she said, "Hide Marshmallow."

She turned back to Rooney. "Don't be scared. They won't hurt you." She had to speak loudly because Rooney was making such a fuss. "They're just ferrets!" Emma called to him. "Not rats. They're on leashes. And they can't hurt you. Honest."

But Rooney didn't believe it. He wanted to get away. And so, it seemed, did every other horse in the barn. Every one of them was awake, whinnying and neighing. They were also banging themselves against the walls of their stalls, as if they wanted to get loose, as if someone had shot off the starter pistol for a race.

And then, lights began popping on. First one. Then another. Followed by a loud ringing sound— an alarm.

And footsteps. Heavy footsteps pounding toward

the barn, coming from the back, where Marcus lived.

Emma looked at Luisa.

Luisa looked at Emma.

They both turned. There was plenty of light now. They fled. Out of the barn. Into the darkness of the woods. Down the hill. Across Luisa's yard. Through the field. Up the slope of Emma's lawn. And into the house through the creaky back door that didn't creak at all this time.

Within minutes, all four of them—Emma, Luisa, Marmaduke, and Marshmallow—were snug in Emma's bed.

Chapter Sixteen
Where Is Emma's Horse?

Even though Emma had been up half the night, she was awake early the next morning. She and Luisa, too. Emma had to get to Graybill's. She had to see how Rooney was and see if he was okay. More than anything, she had to see if he was even there. Or if horrible Oliver had already come and bought him and hauled him away.

Emma put both ferrets back into their cages. She gave them some food, but they didn't seem interested. Emma thought they were probably exhausted from last night just like she was. Right away, they both turned 'round and 'round, settling in for sleep.

Marshmallow didn't seem at all bothered that he'd been stuck in the dryer vent. Emma called it Marshmallow's "near-death" experience, although she knew she was exaggerating. Still, it had a nice sort of dramatic sound to it. Emma had decided not to clean off the baby oil the night before, because Marshmallow definitely looked more like a rat with the oil on her.

The only thing was, with all of Marshmallow's baby oil, Emma's bed got awfully slimy. So did Emma and Luisa. And Marmaduke.

So what? They'd clean up later.

Now, Emma and Luisa ran downstairs, ready to head up to Graybill's. Mom was already in the kitchen, still in her bathrobe, leaning against the counter, her eyes half closed, waiting for her coffee to brew. Before Mom had her morning coffee, she acted like one of those walking-dead zombie people you see in movies. Now, she just smiled sleepily at Emma and Luisa.

"Morning, Mrs. O'Fallon," Luisa said.

Mom sort of waved hello.

"We'll be back in a minute," Emma said.

"Wait. Where are you going?" Mom said.

Where were they going? Emma had a feeling that Mom wouldn't want her to go to Graybill's so early, especially since Annie didn't work there on Saturdays.

So Emma told her first lie of the day, although it wasn't a bad lie. "To Luisa's," Emma said. "We'll be right back."

Mom nodded. "Okay." She sighed. "But you need breakfast."

"Right. Be right back," Emma said.

At the back door, Emma and Luisa stopped. It had rained after their trip, and the horse fields would be really disgusting. Emma had already regretted that she and Luisa had worn just sneakers, not boots, the night before. Their sneakers were covered in mud. If you were going to hang around a barn, you definitely needed boots.

Luckily, there were some rain boots by the door. Emma didn't have real riding boots, but maybe she'd get some, now that Daddy had said she could have riding lessons. Her rain boots were shiny rubber, blue with green frogs on them.

There was also a pair of McClain's boots, pink with yellow rubber duckies. Emma handed the duckie ones to Luisa. "Try these," Emma said. "I think they'll fit."

Luisa sat down and pulled at them. Emma could see that it was a tight fit, but with some tugging and squeezing and puffing, Luisa managed to get them on.

"Good thing I have baby-sized feet," Luisa said. She stood up. "Okay, ready."

Once again, they headed out across the field, through Luisa's yard, and up the hill.

At Graybill's, some horses were grazing out in the corral, but Emma noted right away that Rooney wasn't among them. In the ring, there were lots of people, mostly girls standing next to their horses. Horrible Katie was one of the girls. But none of those horses was Rooney, either. An instructor was walking around, checking the horses' saddles and girths and stirrups and everything.

"Look what Katie's wearing," Emma whispered to Luisa.

Luisa looked and made a face.

Katie was dressed in the full outfit of a professional rider—a professional rider or a really spoiled kid: canvas riding pants with leather or something down the sides, a red jacket, a hard black felt helmet that looked brand new with the strap tucked under her chin, and brown riding boots. Emma knew— because she'd been at horse supply places with Annie—that those boots cost probably two hundred dollars. Katie looked as if she were going to be in a horse movie. And she must have been about dying in the heat, too.

"Oh, Emma! Luisa!" Katie cried. "Come here, come over here! Did you hear what happened last night?"

Emma snuck a sideways look at Luisa. Yes. She knew exactly what had happened last night. But she wanted to hear what Katie had to say.

Emma and Luisa walked over to the ring. Katie

was holding her horse's reins in one hand and was leaning back against her horse. Emma knew you shouldn't do that. Horses weren't meant to be leaning posts.

"What?" Emma asked, all innocent like. "What happened?"

"Someone tried to steal some horses!" Katie said. "In the middle of the night. Marcus said he almost caught him, but the guy must have been scared off by the alarm."

"Did Marcus see him?" Emma asked. She thought she knew the answer to that, too. At least, she hoped she knew the answer—that he hadn't seen her and Luisa. "He didn't steal Rooney, did he?"

Katie shook her head. "Didn't steal any horses. But he tried. He probably wouldn't have bothered stealing Rooney. I know you like Rooney, but nobody else wants him. He's old."

"Some people want him," Emma said. She didn't know why she said that, but she hated Katie insulting Rooney. "Somebody's coming to look at him today."

Katie shook her head. "They already came. And left. They didn't want him."

Emma slid a look at Luisa. She wanted to laugh and yell. Yippee!

Before Emma could say a word, Katie said, "I like

your boots, Emma. Yours too, Luisa. They're so
. . . cute. Childish."

"*So are you,*" Emma said. But she said it only
inside her head.

"And you know what else?" Katie went on. "That
family who came this morning didn't buy Rooney
because he's too old, and nobody wants an old
horse. Really. Nobody. So if Marcus can't sell him,
I bet anything he'll put Rooney down."

"*Put him down!?* You mean, like, *kill* him?"
Emma said.

"Well, you don't have to say it *that* way," Katie
said.

"But that's what it means!" Emma said. "And
you're wrong. Marcus would never do that!"

"He might," Katie said. "What do you think they
do with old horses? They kill them and sell them
to a meat factory and make dog food out of them.
That's what my dad told me. That's why he bought
me a young horse."

"You're lying!" Emma said. But her heart was
beating wildly, and she felt as terrified as she'd
ever felt in her whole life. Even more terrified than
yesterday when Marshmallow was stuck in the
dryer vent.

Katie shrugged. "So don't believe me. But I heard
Marcus talking to those people about Rooney. They

even argued. The people said he was too old and Marcus was asking too much money for such an old horse, and an old horse like him wasn't worth anything anyway."

"Where's Rooney now?" Emma asked.

Katie just shrugged.

Emma felt weak, like she needed to sit down. It was the same feeling she'd had that time in first grade when she had to sing all by herself in front of the whole school.

"That's a big lie, Katie," Luisa said. "You shouldn't say things you don't know anything about. They used to do that with old horses, but not anymore. There're laws against that."

Emma turned to Luisa. Were there really? Or was Luisa just saying that to be nice?

"All right, girls!" It was the riding instructor calling. He clapped his hands. "Come on. Mount up."

Katie turned away and started to mount her horse. Emma noticed that she wasn't doing it very well. The stirrup was too high. She should have had a box to stand on. She put one foot in the stirrup and tried to throw her leg over the back of her horse. It didn't work. She dropped down again.

Emma couldn't see Katie's face, but from the way her neck got red, Emma could tell that Katie was embarrassed.

112

Emma wasn't sure why she did what she did next. But she jumped over the fence into the ring. She folded her hands together the way Marcus had done for her and gave Katie a boost up on top of her horse. For one second, Emma was tempted to keep on boosting Katie up till she fell off the other side of the horse. But Emma didn't do it.

Katie settled herself. She muttered something. Maybe it was even "Thanks." She sure didn't say it very loud. She clicked her tongue, picked up the reins, dug in her heels, and trotted off.

Emma climbed out of the ring and turned to Luisa.

"Don't worry," Luisa said. "Katie was lying. Honest. They don't do that anymore. There're laws against it."

"You just saying that?" Emma asked. "Or do you know it?"

Luisa looked away. It's what she always did when she was lying. Still, Emma knew it was a nice lie. "Let's go find Rooney," Luisa said, taking Emma's arm. "He's here. I know he is."

This time, Luisa didn't look as if she were lying.

Chapter Seventeen
Injured!

Emma and Luisa ran into the barn and right to Rooney's stall.

No Rooney.

They walked up and down the rows of stalls. He wasn't there.

They went outside and looked in the far corral. No Rooney.

And then Emma saw Marcus in the field, way back near his own house. He was loading some hay into his rickety pickup truck.

Emma raced down the hill toward him, Luisa running alongside.

"Marcus!" Emma said, coming to a breathless halt. "Marcus, where's Rooney?"

Marcus tilted his head. "Out back. There," he said.

"Where?" Emma asked.

"Back of my house. Resting."

"Oh," Emma said. What did he need to rest from? Last night? Or the Oliver kid?

"Mighty wild goings-on around here last night," Marcus said, scowling.

"I heard," Emma said. She couldn't meet Marcus' eyes. She had a sudden thought that he could tell just by looking at her that the "goings-on" were connected in some way to her and Luisa. She bent over her boots, pretending to scrape off some mud. "Katie told me."

"You didn't have nothing to do with that, the two of you, did you, now?" Marcus said, as if he were reading her mind. "Did you decide to come visit Rooney?"

Luisa shook her head. She slid a look at Emma.

"We were asleep!" Emma said. She still couldn't look up. "It was nighttime. That's when Katie said it all happened."

Marcus didn't say anything more.

Emma suddenly felt awful. What she had done was wrong. Not only scaring Rooney, but keeping Marcus up half the night. But she'd make it up to Marcus. Somehow. Maybe help muck out the barns.

Marcus turned back and began loading hay into his truck again. The bales seemed to be very heavy, and he was sweating. Emma also thought she heard him swearing a little under his breath.

Emma looked at Luisa. Luisa looked back. Emma had to ask about Oliver. And about Rooney being dog meat. But she couldn't get the words out.

She just stood there next to Marcus for what seemed like a very long time.

Finally, Marcus dropped the last bale of hay into the truck. "What?" he said. "What are you two hanging around for?"

Emma shrugged. "Nothing. I mean"—she sucked in her breath. She still couldn't ask about dog food and horse meat—"I mean, how come that Oliver kid didn't buy Rooney?"

"I wouldn't sell to that kid. Not if you gave me a million bucks."

"You wouldn't? But you said—"

"He took Rooney out for a ride. Rooney came back, all lathered up, his mouth all sore, the mouthpiece and bit pulled this way and that. His mouth was even bleeding. I don't sell horses to folks like that. Told them folks that Rooney cost ten thousand dollars."

"He does?" Emma asked. "Really?"

Marcus laughed. "'Course not. Maybe six hundred. They wouldn't pay ten thousand dollars for no old horse. They were mighty perturbed. Said I'd lied in the ad. Well, what if I did? Like I'd sell Rooney to some kid who'd mistreat him!"

"Katie said you were going to kill him," Emma blurted out. "Kill Rooney, I mean. Not Oliver." She hadn't meant to say it that way. But what other way was there? "'Cause he's so old. But you won't do that, will you? Katie was lying, right?"

"*Who* told you that?" Marcus asked.

"Katie," Luisa said.

"Who's Katie?" Marcus said.

"Just a girl," Emma said. "She rides here."

"Not for long, she don't," Marcus said. "Not if she keeps talking like an idiot."

Emma looked at Luisa. Luisa looked at Emma. Emma was so relieved. Marcus wouldn't sell Rooney to anyone who'd mistreat him. Rooney wouldn't get killed. He might still get sold, though.

"Horses," Marcus said, shaking his head and speaking so softly, it was almost as if he were talking to himself. "They're my life. I don't got much, but I got horses. Anyone who loves horses, they got my respect." He nodded at Emma as if he were including her in the ones who loved horses. "And them that don't," he added, "they don't ride my horses. They can ride somewhere else."

Marcus reached into the front seat of his truck and took out a scrunched-up paper bag. He handed it to

Emma. It smelled of apples—end-of-summer apples.

"Here. Give a few of these to Rooney," Marcus said. "These will be soft on his mouth. He's in that field behind the house. I think he'll be happy to see you."

Chapter Eighteen
Emma's Big, Big Decision

When Emma finished hugging Rooney and giving him his apples, she and Luisa headed home. Emma was pretty exhausted from all the worry and excitement. In front of Luisa's house, Emma saw that there was a mess of stuff outside in the yard and in the driveway.

YARD SALE/GARAGE SALE, a sign said. MOVING SALE. EVERYTHING MUST GO!

There were old toys and cooking pots and clothing and books and games set out on tables. There was a rocking horse that Emma and Luisa used to play on, and a dollhouse that they once sat on, making it collapse—but Luisa's dad had fixed it.

A whole line of cars was parked in the street. People were walking up and down between the tables that had been set out. Emma looked around at all the stuff. Sometimes she went with Annie to garage sales, and usually, she liked them. But now, she hated seeing all of Luisa's things set out like this.

Luisa's mom was sitting at a table, counting out some change.

"Hi, Mrs. P!" Emma called.

"Hi, Emma!" Mrs. Parasullo called back. "Did you girls have a nice evening together?"

Emma and Luisa exchanged looks.

"We did!" Emma said.

"We did!" Luisa echoed. "Nice and quiet," she said softly to Emma.

"Luisa," Mrs. P said. "I'd like you home soon. Your dad and I could use a little help here."

"Okay," Luisa said. "I have to get my backpack at Emma's, though."

"And have breakfast!" Emma said. She really didn't want Luisa to leave yet.

"Okay," Mrs. P said. "But then come home. Emma, you can come, too, if you'd like."

Emma and Luisa went back to Emma's house. At the back door, they sat on the steps, pulling off their muddy boots.

"Luisa?" Emma said. "When are you moving?"

Luisa shrugged. "I don't know. Pretty soon, I guess."

"But I don't want you to!" Emma said. "You're

my best friend. Who else would go with me to see Rooney and play soccer and rescue Marshmallow—and everything?"

"You're my best friend, too," Luisa said. "But maybe I can see you in school. If we don't move too far away."

"Why can't you stay in the house till your dad gets a job?"

"'Cause the bank won't let us," Luisa said. "Mom and Daddy said that some things you own, and some you don't own yet. I don't have to worry about my toys and books and clothes, because we own them unless I feel like selling stuff at the garage sale. But we don't *own* the house—we have a mortgage. And since Daddy lost his job, he hasn't been able to pay what we owe the bank, so the bank is taking the house back."

Emma thought that was the saddest thing she'd ever heard. "That stinks," Emma said. "I hate that bank."

"Everything stinks!" Luisa said. Her eyes had gotten shiny, and she turned her head away. She sucked in a kind of trembly breath. "Let's go," she said, and she got to her feet. "Let's get my stuff."

Upstairs, the little kids were awake and running all over the place. Emma could hear them jumping up and down on Mom and Daddy's bed.

"Mom?" Emma called. "I'm going back to Luisa's. Okay? I'm going to help with their garage sale."

"Okay!" Mom called. She sounded awake by now, as if the coffee had worked. "Did you get any breakfast?"

"We'll take it with us!" Emma said.

She and Luisa went to the kitchen. Emma took some yoghurt from the refrigerator, and Luisa got some bananas and apples from the fruit bowl.

They took them over to Luisa's house.

For the rest of the day, Emma worked alongside Luisa and her mom and dad. It was kind of fun, actually. They sold lots of stuff. Luisa was allowed to keep the money from any toys or books that were sold. But her parents kept the money from the clothes that Luisa had outgrown.

They worked all day, till about six o'clock. Now that it was late summer, it began to get dark earlier. In the dim light, Luisa counted out her money. She had made twenty-seven dollars and sixty-four cents.

Emma thought about it a while.

Ferret food cost ten dollars for a big bag. It lasted Emma's ferrets for a couple of weeks. So for twenty-seven dollars, Luisa could have . . . well, Emma wasn't very good at math. But maybe Luisa would have enough money for three or even four months of food. And Marshmallow had been given all her shots. So there would be no vet bills. And she had a nice, big cage.

And besides—besides, Marshmallow loved Luisa, maybe even Marshmallow loved Luisa best of all. And Luisa loved her back. If Luisa had a wonderful ferret to love, it might not matter so much if she didn't have a house. Right?

Emma turned toward home. "I'll be back in a minute," she told Luisa.

She ran up to her room. She took Marshmallow out of her cage. She kissed her little shiny nose.

For the first time in a while, Marshmallow kissed her back. "Good-bye," Emma whispered to her. "Have fun with Luisa. Make her happy, okay?"

Marshmallow nodded.

Emma took one of the bags of ferret food and tucked it under her arm. Then she carried Marshmallow, the cage, and the food downstairs, across the back field, and around to the front where Luisa was helping her mom and dad close things up.

"Here," Emma said, handing over the cage, the food, and Marshmallow, too. "I want you to have Marshmallow."

"Have her?" Luisa said, smiling. "For tonight? Oh, thanks!"

"No!" Emma said, and she shook her head. "No.

123

Not just for tonight. For good. She needs a . . . home. With you."

"Really? I mean, do you mean it? Thank you, thank you!" Luisa said. "But, but Emma . . . Emma, won't you miss her?"

Emma nodded. "Uh, huh. And I'll miss you, too."

And then, without another word—because she couldn't speak—Emma turned around and ran home.

Tears blurred her eyes. But it was okay. It was. At least, it was okay enough.

Or maybe not.

Chapter Nineteen
Everything Stinks

Emma was dreaming. Fire engines were in her driveway, their engines mumbling and rumbling. Emma's bed felt as if it were trembling.

She sat up.

The sun was shining. It was morning. And it wasn't a dream.

Emma jumped out of bed and looked outside. Two firefighters were walking around, talking to Daddy and Tim. One firefighter had taken off his helmet and was wiping his bald head with a big handkerchief. Daddy was laughing. Tim was laughing, too.

Well, there sure couldn't be much of a fire if they were laughing about it. But then, why were the firefighters there?

Emma threw on shorts and a T-shirt and ran down the stairs and outside.

Mom was sitting on the back steps, her coffee mug in her hand.

"What happened?" Emma asked.

"Oh, nothing much," Mom said. "Don't be worried. Just some smoke from the dryer vent. But it was only smoke. No fire."

"Oh," Emma said. She swallowed hard.

The little kids had come running out at almost the same time Emma had. Annie was right behind.

"Everything all right?" Annie asked.

Mom nodded. "It is. I put a load of wash in the dryer, turned it on, and everything went kaput. Seems like the dryer just blew out. But there was smoke, so Daddy called 911."

"Did you drop and roll?" McClain asked. "That's what you're supposed to do in a fire, drop and roll. We learned that at school. Remember when we had a fire in your house, Annie?"

Annie laughed. "I do remember," she said. "Practically my first week with you."

Emma remembered, too. That had been her fault, Emma's fault. She had turned on the oven by mistake in Annie's apartment, instead of turning on the burner to make tea. Annie had her passport hidden in the oven and it had smoked up the place something awful. Annie's passport was ruined. But Annie had never told Mom that it was Emma's fault.

Now Emma had done it again.

It was the baby oil. She was sure of it.

"Well, it's not a big deal," Mom said. "That dryer was pretty old anyway. It's washed a lot of kids' clothes and diapers. Shall we all go in and get breakfast now?"

Everyone trooped into the house, and the fire engines and the firefighters went away. It was Sunday, and even though Annie didn't usually work for the family on Sundays, she sometimes helped out or ate with them. Now, Annie was humming and giggling with the little ones. Emma figured that meant Annie was happy, that she and Bo had made up after their tiff.

Daddy was happy, too. He said he'd just received the electric bill, and they had saved two hundred dollars this month! That meant that they'd used lots less electricity and had done a good deed for the environment. They'd taken better care of the earth.

Well, at least there were a few things Emma could be glad about. But everything else stunk, just as Luisa had said. It really stunk. She didn't know if she'd done the right thing by giving Marshmallow away. She felt guilty about the dryer. And Rooney still might get sold, although Emma felt better when she thought about him costing only six hundred dollars. Why that should make her feel better, she didn't know. She didn't have six hundred dollars, and she sure didn't have a couple of thousand dollars a year to care for him.

As Annie helped Mom set the table and played with the little kids, Emma was very quiet. There was only one thing she felt like doing: She wanted to climb a tree and think. In Maine, she always sat in trees. But there were really no good-sized "thinking" trees around here to sit in. Her new tree outside the window wasn't big enough for sitting in yet.

"Emma," Daddy said, looking across the table at her after they were all seated. "You're quiet this morning."

Emma nodded.

"Tired?" Daddy said.

Again, Emma nodded.

"Anything else wrong?" Daddy asked.

Emma shook her head. She wanted to tell. But she'd cry if she did.

All the kids suddenly became quiet. They were looking at her. Emma knew why—the usual. None of the kids liked any of the other kids to be sad. Even McClain could be sweet when someone else was worried. Tim especially was sending her worried looks.

"Don't want to talk about it?" Daddy asked.

Emma shook her head. She felt the tears welling up in her eyes. "I'll be right back," she said.

She ran up to her room. She went to her desk and got out the kitty purse. She brought it downstairs.

She sat down, sliding the purse over to Daddy. "There's sixty dollars in there," she said. "You can have it."

Daddy looked at Emma. He looked at Mom, then back to Emma. "Why, sweetie?" he asked.

"For the dryer," Emma said. "I broke it."

"Oh, honey," Mom said. "No you didn't. That dryer was ten years old. It was time for it to give out. Do you know how many diapers it's dried?"

"I poured baby oil into it," Emma said. "I mean, not into the dryer. Into the vent."

Mom frowned. "You did? Why?"

"To get Marshmallow out. She got stuck in the vent, but the baby oil loosened her up."

Mom and Daddy looked at one another across the table.

"When did this happen, Sweetie?" Daddy asked quietly.

"Day before yesterday. I didn't think it would break the dryer or anything. But it must have leaked in."

"Oh," Daddy said.

"And something else," Emma said. "I gave Marshmallow away."

"You *what?*"

Both Mom and Daddy said it at the same time.

Emma nodded. She swallowed hard. "I gave her to Luisa. Luisa's moving, you know. She doesn't have a house anymore."

"Oh, honey!" Mom said, reaching out and taking Emma's hand. "That was so sweet of you. But oh, you must be sad!"

Tears filled Emma's eyes, and she noticed that there were tears in Mom's eyes, too.

"I am sad," Emma said. "And I'm scared. What if Marshmallow thinks I gave her away because I didn't like her anymore? Maybe she feels like she doesn't have a home, either, and maybe I shouldn't have, and anyway, everything's wrong."

Daddy pushed his chair back from the table. He held out his arms. "Come here, sweetheart," he said.

Mom let go of Emma's hand, and Emma got up and went around the table.

Daddy took her into his lap. He held her head against his chest. He began rocking her a little, like she was just a tiny kid, no bigger than Ira or Lizzie.

"You did the right thing," Daddy whispered. "You really did."

McClain got up and came around the table, too. Also Woof. Emma still had her head pressed against Daddy's chest, so she wasn't able to see much.

But she felt Woof put his big head in her lap. And McClain began patting Emma's head very, very softly. For some weird reason, that made Emma cry even more.

She cried for everything—for Marshmallow and Rooney and Luisa and Luisa's daddy losing his job and Luisa losing her house.

She cried because it seemed that nobody had a safe place or home anywhere anymore.

Chapter Twenty
Almost Perfect

"Don't worry, me dears. Things will be better in the morning."

Annie had said that the night of the thunderstorm when they had all snuggled together in her apartment. And it was true. It had been true the morning after the storm, and it was true this morning.

It was Monday, Emma's last week at soccer camp. And before the sun was even up, Daddy came into her room.

"Wake up, Sweetie," he said, touching her shoulder. "I have a surprise for you."

Emma sat up and blinked. "What?"

"Get dressed. I'll be waiting for you outside. We're going somewhere special."

"We are? Oh," Emma said. She rubbed her eyes.

"Am I going to camp?"

"Later," Daddy said. "But first, I have a surprise. So get dressed."

Emma tumbled out of bed. She pulled on her clothes for camp. She was too sleepy to bother with sneakers. She just picked up her flip-flops and stumbled downstairs.

Mom was in the kitchen, that sleepy, dopey, I-haven't-had-my-coffee look on her face, but she smiled when Emma came in. "Daddy and I cooked up a plan," Mom whispered as she gave Emma a hug. "I'm staying here with the kiddos. You go with Daddy."

"Where?" Emma asked.

"You'll see," Mom said. "Scoot."

Outside, Emma found Daddy waiting in the car. "I'm taking you to breakfast," he said. "Just you and me. But we have something to do first."

"What?" Emma said. She climbed in the backseat and rubbed her eyes. She could barely get her eyes open. "Why so early?"

"I have to work this week," Daddy said. "I'll be on my plane in a few hours."

"Oh," Emma said.

When they left the driveway, Daddy didn't turn into town toward a restaurant. Instead, he headed up the hill to Graybill's. A car couldn't go to the barns the way Emma and Luisa went—through the fields and woods. Daddy drove the long way around, although it took only a minute or two.

Soon they were bumping up the windy, pitted drive. Emma was beginning to wake up fast. What was happening?

"Daddy?" she said. "What are we doing here?"

Daddy didn't answer. He just pulled up and parked by the barns. "Come on," he said. "You'll wake up in a minute. Let's get out."

He opened the back door for Emma. She climbed out, and he took her hand. Together they walked around back to Marcus' house, Emma being careful about where she stepped. Flip-flops weren't much good when there was horse poop everywhere.

When they got behind the house, there was Rooney—still there, in his own private corral. Marcus was standing by him, holding a pail of oats or treacle or something.

Marcus turned when he heard them coming. He nodded at them.

"Morning, Marcus!" Daddy said.

Marcus nodded again but didn't answer. Emma was used to that. It seemed that Marcus never said a word if he could avoid it.

"How's Rooney doing today?" Daddy asked.

"Mouth is healing," Marcus said. "A good solid horse, he is. And again, I thank you so much. That I do."

"For what?" Emma asked, looking up at Daddy.

"Mom and I bought Rooney," Daddy said.

Emma blinked at him. She took a step back. "I don't believe you," she said. "You said I couldn't have a horse. You said—"

"Forget what I said," Daddy said. "Parents can change their minds, you know. Mom and I have given it a lot of thought. Rooney needs a home. Marcus is happy to give him a good home. And you want to ride Rooney. So we're paying that lady, Ms. Adams, six hundred dollars."

"*You're* paying for him?" Emma said.

Daddy nodded.

"Then that means . . . does that mean he's mine?" Emma said. "I own him? We own him?"

"No," Daddy said. "He's not yours. He's Marcus' horse now. And Marcus is going to care for him— feed him and shoe him and exercise him, all those things a horse needs and that Marcus does so well." Daddy smiled. "And you'll help out around the barns in exchange for the lessons Marcus will give you. We haven't figured out all the details yet, but we will."

Emma looked at Daddy. Her heart had begun

doing funny things inside her, like it was bursting to get out.

She turned to Marcus.

She turned to Rooney. Rooney was poking his big head over the rail, waiting for her to hug and kiss him.

Emma turned back to Marcus. He was actually smiling.

"Never seen a young'un take to a horse like you do," Marcus said. "Figure you'll help me care for him just fine."

"I will," Emma said. "Oh, I will. I'll take such good care of him. Honest."

And I'll never again scare him with a ferret.

And then Emma remembered the first day she had ridden Rooney—well, the first time she had been *allowed* to ride him, not just steal a ride on him. She remembered how she had hugged Rooney. And how she had thought that, if it wasn't so embarrassing, she'd have hugged Marcus, too.

Well, right now she didn't care about being embarrassed. She took a deep breath. Then, she threw her arms around Marcus and hugged him.

He didn't hug her back. He just patted her shoulder a little.

Then Emma looked at Daddy. She threw herself into his arms, hugging him, too. "Thanks, Daddy, oh, thank you so, so much!" she whispered. "You're the best."

"No, *you're* the best," Daddy whispered. "And I love you to pieces."

Emma turned away. She climbed up on the rail and leapt down into the corral. She stood on tiptoes and threw her arms up and around Rooney's neck.

Rooney pressed against her. He almost knocked her over, giving her his big, fat horse hug.

For a long while they stood that way. Emma felt sure that Rooney had listened to all that had been said. And she knew that he was happy. He had a home, a home with Marcus who loved him and Emma who loved him, and . . .

And Emma thought of something else. She thought that maybe that's what home was—not a house or an apartment or even a barn, but a place where people loved you most of all. And if that were true, then not just Rooney, but Marshmallow—and even Luisa—could be happy.

Emma glanced at Marcus and Daddy. Daddy was smiling at her. Marcus was smiling at her.

And, although Emma couldn't be exactly sure, she was pretty sure that Rooney was smiling, too.